# Spirit

# of

# Christmas

# Cyberworld Publishing

**www.cyberworldpublishing.com**

ISBN 978-0-9808011-6-3

Cyberworld Publishing *publisher*
*Jindalee St, Toronto, Australia*

# Books By Olivia Stowe

Spirit of Christmas

Chatham Square

By the Howling

Retired With Prejudice

Fiddler's Rest

# Spirit of Christmas

## Olivia Stowe

# Table of Contents

# Preface

The Christmas season reawakens the desires and encouragement to give of oneself and to help others in need. For thirty-five years I have created my own Christmas cards, painting each one separately, not because I have any pretensions about my artistic abilities, but to convey to the receiver that I have spent the time and effort to create something for each of those on my card list and to share some theme that the year has highlighted in my life. For the last several years I have also included a story that follows the theme of the card. This anthology includes fifteen of those stories. Not all of them deal specifically with a Christmas theme, but all of them attempt to capture the essence of the spirit of Christmas—a spirit, I believe, that is worth retaining and practicing all the year through.

This collection provides an opportunity for those conflicted in various ways or swept up in the hustle and bustle of holiday routine to pause, contemplate, grasp, and be heartened and set in motion by the true spirit of the season.

These stories share an element of unexpected gifts or struggling to "catch on" to what the season is all about. In "Blue

Christmas" the gift is a young man's call home, in "How Big the Ocean," it is one of companionship and good humor in the face of adversity. "Betsy's Birds" bestows the gift of a sense of true community, and "Fading Star's" gift hinges on a jarring medical diagnosis. The gifts of "The Italian Crèche" and "The Gift" are ones of selfless sacrifice and "Time for Grace" unwraps the gift of social consciousness. "Clyde Saves Christmas" provides a whimsical cat's-eye view of gift giving, while "Timing Out" grew out of frustration at world events of the time, and "Moment of the Deer" provides a much more serious jolt to a woman's system on what the Christmas spirit is all about.

The stories, themselves Christmas gifts, are meant to be great mood lifters for those who feel overwhelmed or marginalized by the commercialism of Christmas. And if some of the themes seem repetitive, note that this is a collection created over more than a dozen years and that the spirit of Christmas isn't really all that complex or hard to discern—it just comes to us in many different circumstances. Thus, the stories might best be enjoyed by savoring them and reading them individually over time as the mood strikes you.

# Spirit of Christmas

"Good morning, Mrs. Stewart. It's good to see you out. How're doin' today?"

"Oh, you know, Mr. Baxter. Each day just sort of nudges the one before it. It just all sort of goes on—a bit too long, if you ask me."

Clem Baxter watched Louise Stewart from 12A move arthritically down the walk between the two old, red-brick apartment houses facing each other. Clem had been the super of these buildings for nearly twenty years, and he knew most of the tenants by their apartment numbers, but he'd grown to know the names of those living in his own hall. Louise turned right when she got to Elm. The Shoprite was in that direction, and Clem saw that she was carrying her shopping bag. He tried to remember when she'd gone to shopping nearly every day and couldn't rightly pin it down. It seemed she was going more often now than when her Johnny was alive. But then maybe she'd been bringing groceries home when she was still working. That had been the two bad things that had happened to Mrs. Stewart since the summer. Her boy had finally died and she'd been retired from her job.

This would be her first Christmas without her boy and her job. Clem sure wished he could do something to cheer her up, but they'd cut his super hours and he was feeling the financial pinch too. Times were tough. Mrs. Johnson in 1GA had her time cut back on her too, and she was trying to raise three small children by herself. And then there was the young couple in 11B, the Wilcoxes— although their problem was that they were barely making it with both of them working and now she was pregnant and would be off for a while and then maybe couldn't go back full time. And that Jim Wilcox was so busy helping at the food bank, he was pretty worn out with the paying job he had on top of that.

Yep, times were tough, Clem thought as he moved back into the hall and entered his apartment, 11A. As he gathered up cleaning supplies to work on the vacant 12B, he heard the knock on the door. When he opened it, the deliveryman was already half way down the sidewalk back to Elm street. Looking down, Clem saw a small Christmas gift basket. The building owners did this every year—gave him a gift basket. He'd rather have a cash bonus, but it was sort of interesting to see what weird things he'd find in these baskets-- including coupons and things like this lottery ticket.

"This lottery ticket," Clem thought. Why did he suddenly think of Mrs. Stewart? Maybe because it was for a Shoprite frozen turkey—advertised as somebody's New Year's Day meal.

To Clem this was fate. He chuckled that fate smiled on even those on the down and out like he and his neighbors. He scrounged around and came up with a stray envelope and printed "Merry Christmas" in a hand he hoped Mrs. Stewart wouldn't recognize, inserted the lottery ticket, hurried up the stairs, and slipped it under her door.

For three days, the lottery ticket dominated Louise Stewart's thoughts as nothing else had done since Johnny died the day after she'd received notice she was being retired. So taken had her thoughts been with the passing of her last reasons for living that when her old refrigerator died, she'd done no more than found a temporary fix of a countertop refrigerator from the Salvation Army store. The lottery ticket brought new, intriguing questions into her life. Who put it under her door and why? Who would give her a present at all? Everyone in her life was gone now. She was all alone.

But could she really say she was all alone when someone had given her a Christmas present—one that captured her attention for three days? The one question she didn't give much thought to—because nothing in life had encouraged her to consider winning a lottery—was what she'd do with the eighteen-pound turkey prize if she won it.

Thus, when she was struggling home on Christmas Eve from Shoprite with her eighteen-pound turkey prize, Louise wasn't considering what she was going to do with it when she had no freezer and not even a refrigerator large enough for it or an oven big enough to cook it in.

These realities did surface in her mind when she was standing at the foot of the stairs up to her floor in the apartment hallway and wondering if the turkey might take a turn in carrying her the last nearly vertical twelve feet. That's when she wondered how big a freezer Pam Wilcox in 11B had.

When Pam answered her door, three observations simultaneously struck Louise. She could see through to the kitchen, where there was a nice big refrigerator with freezer and, as a bonus, a stove with an oven that looked like it could hold an eighteen-pound turkey. And in the foreground was a young lady who looked like she was eleven months pregnant with triplets—a young lady who wasn't at work.

In a flash, Louise remembered that Pam's forced maternity leave had started two days earlier and that she and her husband were worried about finances now. The grief of Louise's own job loss and all that it had entailed welled up in her. She had intended only to ask if Pam had room in her freezer to hold the turkey until Louse could decide what to do with it, but that's not what she said when Pam opened the door. Instead, she said "Merry Christmas" and pressed the turkey into Pam's arms and turned and started climbing the stairs.

Pam stammered in surprise, unable to form her words, and Louise filled the gap with a decisive, "You two have a feast for New Year's, dear. You are going to need the strength very soon now."

She was through the door of 12A and standing and chuckling—or hyperventilating, she couldn't be sure which—while Pam was still standing in her doorway, flapping her jaw and feeling the cold in a peculiar place. "What an interesting Christmas present that was," Louise whispered before she took her two-day's worth of groceries into her kitchen.

"What's the matter, Jim?" Pam asked two days later as the two were sitting at the dinner table. "You've been glum for a week now. Christmas should be a time of joy, and we're about to have our

14

own bundle of joy." For two days Pam had been avoiding saying much of anything to Jim. She was afraid of what might be worrying him so much. Second thoughts of fatherhood or deep worry about the loss of her income? It could be either or both, and neither was something she wanted to give voice to.

"It's because it's Christmas," he answered. "The cupboard is practically bare down at the food bank. There are going to be families without enough to eat for New Year's. And remember how I pledged that our big spending for Christmas was going to be helping the food bank? I just don't see now that—"

"Hold that thought for a moment, love," Pam said. She stood up and went to the refrigerator and opened the freezer door. She did so rather reluctantly. She'd looked forward to a special New Year's meal. But they would manage. She remembered how excited Jim had been when he'd come up with the idea of this special Christmas pledge he wanted to make and how relieved he'd been and the love he'd shown when she readily went along with the scheme. She knew how much the food bank effort meant to him—and how much he meant to her.

It had been a very nice present from Louise Stewart, one that had touched Pam deeply—so deeply that she hadn't found the right time to tell Jim about it yet.

The surprise in Jim's face when she plopped the eighteen-pound turkey on the table in front of him, not to mention and awe and love she saw in his eyes when she told him that could be their contribution to the food bank, was worth the most expensive Christmas present Pam could think of—and Pam gave a little prayer of thanksgiving for Louise Stewart's gift as she watched Jim march off to the food bank with the turkey in his hands.

As Jim Wilcox was arriving at the food bank and wondering who of the many client families they had that could make best use of the turkey, Sarah Johnson was leaving the basement apartment 1GA to make the first trip she had ever made to the food bank. She had been signed up for their services for several months now, but up to this time pride and the determination to handle her problems herself had kept her from making that trip to the food bank. But there had been one thing she really wanted to do this Christmas season, and it was growing almost too late to do it. Thus, she had swallowed her pride and asked Mrs. Stewart in 12A if she could sit for the children while she went on an errand, and Sarah had built up the courage to venture forth.

Jim Wilcox saw Sarah Johnson coming through the door of the food bank—slowly and hesitatingly—and he knew immediately where the turkey would go. He had been meaning to encourage her to come in; he knew the Johnsons were backsliding, and he'd even had thoughts to telling her that he'd bring a food basket to her before Christmas, even though this was not covered in the organization's rules. She had signed up, though, and whereas other client families had been receiving food aid, she'd hadn't done so yet.

The turkey wouldn't be above and beyond what she had a right to receive in services this Christmas season.

He saw her turn, indecisive, possibly to exit right after she entered, and he moved quickly forward and put his hand on her arm.

"Please, please, do come in Mrs. Johnson. We have something for you. You were on the books for something for a

Christmas meal and you didn't come. We'll be pleased if you take a basket for New Year's. There's one right over here. I just have to put something else in it and it will be ready for you."

Sarah Johnson's eyes went big and watery as she saw Jim Wilcox struggle out of the back room with an eighteen-pound frozen turkey and plop it in a box with other staples for a holiday meal.

"But . . . but . . . Mr. Wilcox. It's so big. I don't think I—"

"Sure you can. I'm sure you can find folks to share your New Year's meal with you."

"Well, since you mention it," she said, her voice suddenly small, "my one wish for Christmas was to have a few others in for a meal this season. I'll take this—but only on condition that you and Mrs. Wilcox join my family for the New Year's Day meal."

"Pam and I? Why I don't know—"

"I was going to ask you anyway. Louise Stewart from upstairs and Mr. Baxter from across the hall from you have already said they'd come—although I didn't promise them a meal as fancy as this will fix. Please come. This was the one thing I was looking forward to for this season. We've all of us—on our hall at the apartments—have had a pretty rough year—but you are about to start a family, and I can tell you what a joy children are even if it's hard to provide for them. I thought we were all due to be able to share a bit of the spirit of Christmas."

# Blue Christmas

"Well, all right, I guess I could do that." Clara tried to make her reluctance quite clear, but Elizabeth was having none of that. She just cheerily plowed along, working on getting Clara on the road to fill in for no-shows among the volunteers at the soup kitchen where Elizabeth was working that evening.

Nothing had put her off—not Clara's remark that it was already dark, not her observation that it had begun to snow—not even the noting that it was Christmas Eve.

Everyone knew Clara didn't come out on Christmas Eve—that she hadn't done so for nearly a decade. Everyone but Elizabeth, apparently. But that wasn't Elizabeth's fault. She'd only moved here last summer, and no one talked about Clara and Christmas Eve any more. And Elizabeth was such a gem. She'd been there for Clara on short notice so many times herself. Clara knew she owed Elizabeth big time, and Elizabeth wasn't being pushy so much as she was assuming that her good friend would do what Elizabeth would do for anyone else in a short-notice bind like this.

Clara couldn't say no—and in the end she didn't. She promised she'd be there. Elizabeth just didn't understand about

Clara and Christmas Eve. Clara knew Elizabeth would be the first one to understand and to be sensitive if she knew.

It started as soon as Clara entered the garage. For some time after that she wondered why she hadn't just stopped trying at that point. As the door into the house shut and locked, Clara realized she didn't have her car keys—or her house keys for that matter. She had an emergency house key hidden in the garage, of course, although it took her a couple of minutes to remember where she'd put it. But she did remember—and in the precious moments she lost in reentering the house and retrieving her car keys and getting the garage door lifted, the snow had begun to stick on the driveway.

"Remember that Elizabeth sounded almost desperate for the help and that she has put everything down to help me so often," Clara muttered to herself as she pulled out of the garage. It would have been hard enough on any snowy night. But it was Christmas Eve. Everyone knew Clara hid away on Christmas Eve. Everyone but Elizabeth. But Elizabeth needed her. She'd said that fewer volunteers had shown up at the soup kitchen than anticipated, but more of the homeless than planned had come in off the street to escape the cold and the snow—and to have some semblance of family on Christmas Eve.

Family on Christmas Eve, Clara thought. And, whether she wanted them to or not, the tears started to roll down her cheeks as she drove out into the dark night.

Clara rolled up to St. Mark's Presbyterian Church on Maple—almost on the other side of town—to find very few cars in the parking lot. This was a surprise, as Elizabeth had said the church was running Christmas programs all evening and their meal and shelter service for the homeless was being hampered by everyone bringing in cookies for the breaks between the church services and competing for counter space in the kitchen.

Clara stepped out of the car—and into a slushy puddle, realizing only then that she hadn't put on her snow boots before she'd left home. And when she got to the door of the church, she found only a group of people finishing putting up the decorations for the late-evening church services.

Clara was almost choked up with the emotion of being in a church for the first time on Christmas Eve in eight years, and it took her several minutes—after having gone into the community building wing and finding the kitchen dark—to build up the capability to return to the sanctuary and query one of those there what the problem was.

"Oh, you must mean St. Mark's Lutheran across town on Landon Street," a cheery, rosy-cheeked woman answered. "I think they are on for the homeless shelter duty over the holidays. We'd be pleased if you attended one of our services here, of course. It's only a little more than an hour before the first of those."

"Uh . . . no thanks," Clara stammered. "Thanks, but no thanks. I don't go to Christmas Eve services anymore. I . . . I can't . . ." By then Clara had backed up to the outer door in the narthex, though, and she turned and fled into the cold, snowy night.

It had been her own fault. She had just latched onto the St. Mark's name when Elizabeth had mentioned where help was needed. Elizabeth probably even had specified it was St. Mark's Lutheran and Clara had been so focused on forming her excuses for not coming that she hadn't paid attention. No wonder Elizabeth thought it wouldn't be much of an imposition, Clara thought. St. Mark's Lutheran was near where Clara had started out from home. Elizabeth had every reason to assume that the snow wouldn't be that much of a problem for Clara.

Clara looked up at the sky. The snowflakes were getting larger and there was increasingly less space between them as they fell. She decided it would be best to take the country road around the perimeter of the town rather than drive through town with all of the rest of the sliding cars.

Bad decision.

Half way around town, on a pitch-black stretch of road going through a thickly forested section, a deer bounded across the road just beyond Clara's headlights and she pulled hard to the right to avoid it. She missed the deer, but she glanced off a boulder at the side of the road with her wheel, and she didn't get more than a couple of hundred yards farther down the road before her tire blew and the car lurched into a side ditch.

"I knew it," Clara moaned. "I knew I shouldn't have tried to come out on Christmas Eve." All of the hurt and frustration and despair of this one night of the year boiled up inside her and Clara was crying again. Big, gasping, gobs of crying—almost wailing. But almost as soon as it had started, it stopped. Clara had controlled herself for eight years; she wasn't going to fall to pieces on Christmas Eve now. She'd call AAA and just get them to take her home. She had borne up under the burden for eight years. She would continue to tough it out.

She was dialing the cell phone under the weak light of the ceiling dome when she heard the tapping on her window.

21

"Can I help?" he asked through the pane of glass.

He looked familiar. Yes, she'd seen him in the group of folks she'd gone to the theater with as Elizabeth's guest the week after Thanksgiving. He'd been sweet. A great smile and funny stories. It had been a group from Elizabeth's church, Clara remembered. She rolled down the window.

"Say, aren't you Mrs. Benton?" he asked.

"Yes, yes," Clara answered. "And you're Ben . . . Ben from Elizabeth Sturges's church group, aren't you?"

"Yes. It looks like you are in a good bit of trouble and that you won't be going anywhere in this car tonight."

"I was just calling AAA," Clara answered.

"Maybe you should do that," Ben answered. "I'd change your tire for you, but it looks like you have some front end damage too."

"I hit a rock—avoiding a deer," Clara said.

"Ah. Well, you can get AAA out here and then I'll drive you anywhere you want to go."

"I don't live that far away," Clara answered. "But where were you headed? I don't want you to be late . . . on Christmas Eve."

"I'm going to church; to St. Mark's on Landon. Helping with some of the church services there this evening."

"Ah," Clara said. She dreaded the thought, but she couldn't forget the help she'd promised to Elizabeth, and her White Knight was headed there already. It seemed to be fate. Clara gave in to it.

"That's where I was originally headed too, actually," Clara admitted. "Elizabeth enlisted me to help with the meal service for the homeless tonight. So, if you want, we could just go there and you could take me home afterward."

"That would be great," Ben said. "You'd even have time to go to a service after the kitchen closed down . . . if you liked."

Clara began to tremble and she barely was able to control her voice when she answered. "I don't really go to Christmas Eve services anymore. If there was someplace I could just wait until you were ready to leave—"

"Sure, sure, no problem," Ben quickly said. And his smile was genuine, so Clara didn't feel she had to make any further excuses.

When they arrived at the church, Elizabeth expressed delight at seeing Clara and clucked sympathetically at the story of how difficult it had been for Clara to get there, but she didn't really seem to be all that much in need of help.

"Some volunteers came in who weren't scheduled," she said. "Just wanted to help out on Christmas Eve. But if you could, Clara, I'd appreciate it if you'd take a meal over to that young man sitting at the table by himself. He didn't come through the food line; just got some coffee, and we'll be closing the line down soon. He looks pretty dejected; I'm sure he needs the meal and a friendly face."

Clara took a tray of food and approached the young man in dread. There was a familiarity about him—even in the way his head was hanging, and his shoulders looked just about ready to collapse into his chest.

"Oh, dear god, not on Christmas Eve," Clara murmured as she approached. On top of everything else she just didn't think she could manage this on Christmas Eve. But she supposed she'd have to.

"Hi," she said.

"Hi to you too," the young man said. When he looked up, there was a familiar sadness in his eyes, and Clara immediately knew that she wouldn't leave him alone. Not on Christmas Eve. She somehow knew this was another chance being given her.

"I brought you some food," she said. And when she set it down on the table at his elbow, she sat down across from him herself. "The kitchen is about to close, and they say you haven't eaten yet."

"Don't need it, thanks. But thanks for bringing it. I'll take the coffee; mine is about all gone."

"Well, maybe you'll feel like eating in a bit," Clara said. "Do you mind if I sit? I've had quite an evening, and it would be good to get off my feet."

"No, it's fine. I don't mind."

Little by little Clara drew the young man out in conversation, and it was no surprise to find that she was right—that the familiar look about him probably meant just what she thought it meant.

When they'd become comfortable with each other and Clara hadn't pressed too much on his evasions—getting only a sketchy "feeling inferior and abandoned by the world" version of why he was here on Christmas Eve rather than anywhere else—she reached down into her pocketbook and took a shiny silver coin out and held it up for the young man to see.

"Would you accept a small Christmas present from me?" she asked softly. "It's not worth much, I'm sure, but I've had it for several years, and I think you might appreciate it. It was my son's."

"Your son's?" the young man asked. He took the coin from her and held it up to the light. "Where's this from?" he asked. "I can't read any of the inscription. It looks fancy, though. What country is it from? And doesn't your son want it anymore?"

"That's the point of it, I think," Clara answered in a low voice that she was using every power she had to keep under control. "Erick's grandfather gave it to him, telling him that it was his job to figure out where it came from—that as long as he had such a quest facing him, he would have a purpose in life."

"Sounds deep," the young man answered. "And why do you have it?"

And then, in faltering but purposeful tones, Clara told the young man, who seemed so similar in his demeanor to her own son, of the Christmas Eve eight years previously when she and her husband had bustled off to church services—not even bothering to listen to why her son, who had been despondent for so long, wasn't going to go with them. And then, how they had come home after midnight to find that he had hanged himself in his room—that he had died, despondent, and all alone on Christmas Eve—while they were at a church service.

"I should have known," Clara said as she at last struggled through the telling of that story. "I was just too busy with getting everything just right for Christmas. But I should have known. I found this coin in the trash can in my bedroom three days before Christmas. I should have known that Erick was trying to reach out to me, was trying to tell me that he had reached the end of whatever hell he was living in. I can only imagine what that was—what it was that would go through the mind of a young man who had everything available to him in life if he just reached out for it. But I'm sure he discarded that coin where he was sure that I'd see it, where I would know that he no longer was seeking. But I was blind. And just too busy getting ready for the season. I . . . I failed him."

Clara looked up at the young man then, into his face. While she'd been telling her story, she hadn't been able to look at him. But now she wanted to know whether he had understood any of this— whether he knew why she had told him a story she'd kept locked inside her for eight years.

And the look he gave her told her that he knew why and that it had to do with him as much as her lost son—but that he was wavering on the fence.

"And your husband?" he whispered.

"He couldn't endure it. We had been living together—but apart—for some time already. He left within a year. And every Christmas since then has been what we call a Blue Christmas for me—the lowest day of the year. And I've never again decorated for Christmas or left my darkened house on Christmas Eve. At least until tonight."

The silence between them was deafening.

But Clara built up the strength to go on. Somehow she knew she had struggled in this evening for a purpose, a purpose that was beyond her control, and that she couldn't leave it this way. She was desperate to move him off that fence. It was as if this was the last chance for her—more so than for the young man.

"I've given you a present now. . . . You'll accept it, won't you? It would mean so much to me."

The young man nodded his head ever so slightly, almost indecisively, but he didn't return the coin.

"So, could I ask for a present from you?" Clara rushed on.

"I don't really have—"

"I have a cell phone here," Clara interrupted. "All I'd like for a present is that you take it and call your parents and tell them you are OK on Christmas Eve. Could you do that for me? You said they didn't live very far from here. Please? I'll move away and give you some privacy."

The young man didn't say no, and Clara put her cell phone on the table in front of him and got up and moved over to Elizabeth before he could turn her request down.

"You certainly seemed to be in serious conversation with that young man," Elizabeth said. From her tone, Clara could tell that Elizabeth was pleased—and maybe relieved. She wouldn't have been surprised to hear that Elizabeth had sought the extra help this evening precisely because of the young man and how sad and desperate he looked.

Clara turned to see that the young man was speaking into the telephone. When she turned back, Elizabeth had retreated into the church's kitchen, where they were beginning to clean up the cooking utensils and making room for an increasing stream of plates of cookies for the festivities between church services upstairs.

Clara followed her into the kitchen, and after several minutes of helping Elizabeth, Clara went back out into the fellowship hall. The young man had finished his call and was standing up.

He handed Clara's cell phone back to her, and she sighed when she saw that the familiar look she'd seen in his face earlier had drained away from him.

"Thanks," he said. "Thank you so much. Could you tell them over at the intake table that I won't be here for the night?"

"You're not going back out into the snow, I hope," Clara said in a concerned voice.

"No. No. My parents are coming by to pick me up in a few minutes. I'll try going home again, I guess."

Tears sprang to Clara's eyes, and she couldn't help beaming up into his face.

"Oh, and . . . um, it's awkward. But could you take this for me? I'm sorry, I don't know what else to do with it. But I don't want it anymore. Don't need it anymore, I think."

As he was saying this, he took a newspaper-wrapped parcel out of his jacket pocket. It made a clunking noise as he put it down on the table.

"And . . . and thanks for the coin. Do you want me to let you know where it came from when I've figured it out?"

"No. No, thanks," Clara answered. "I do believe I'd like to keep it in the seeking mode."

Clara and Elizabeth were slipping through the narthex of the church after leaving the young man's parcel in the pastor's office with a note attached, nervous and not knowing what else to do with the gun the young man had left behind, when Ben came through the door to the sanctuary, which was already nearly filled with people

28

attending the next-to-last evening service. Strains of "It Came Upon a Midnight Clear" were filtering through the church as an introit into the service.

"Oh, there you are, Clara," Ben said. "Come, I'll show you where you can wait and rest until the service is over. I'll be able to take you home after this service."

"Thank you," Clara said, "But if you don't mind, I think maybe I'll come into the service with you. I haven't been out of the house on Christmas Eve, let alone to a Christmas service, in eight years."

As soon as she uttered those words, Clara was sorry that she'd said them in Elizabeth's hearing. Now Elizabeth might learn why and feel bad that she'd brought Clara out on Christmas Eve.

But Elizabeth was at Clara's elbow and was giving a little tentative half smile. "I know you didn't, Clara. I'd heard about that. But I thought it was time that you did come out on this, of all, nights. I hope I—"

Elizabeth didn't have to finish her sentence, though, because Clara smiled and wrapped her arm under Elizabeth's and guided her into the sanctuary behind Ben, looking for three empty spaces in the overflowing pews.

# The Italian Crèche

Emily stopped at her bureau in the sleeping L off her living space while en route to the kitchenette to warm Margaret's tea. She couldn't help herself. She had to open the top drawer just enough to be able to pull out the old worn coin purse and check inside one more time. With the check her nephew, Jonathan, had sent her for Christmas she just might have enough now. And just in time. At least she'd have enough if they had taken their prices down again. This was the last time they'd do so before Christmas, though. It was already the morning of Christmas Eve. Well, if not today, maybe in the after-Christmas sales, she thought—if she was lucky.

Yes it was all there. More than she'd been able to save before. It was such a silly thing to do as much as she had to pinch her pennies, but she'd known ever since it went into the window at Mulberry Junction down in the center of the town in early November that she had to have it. And she'd been holding her breath ever since for fear that someone else decided they also had to have it before she could save enough.

"Are you OK?" Margaret called out from the living area. Margaret had been such a fussbudget ever since Emily had taken that tumble in the early fall. But it was rather nice to have someone fuss over you. Emily hadn't had much of anyone to fuss over her since her parents had been taken together in that flood on the Hughes River—more than fifty years ago now. My, how time flies, Emily thought, with a sigh, as she gently pressed the drawer shut and turned toward her friend.

"Yes, I'm fine, thanks. I was just checking. Now, if only—"

"I'm sure it's still there," Margaret said. "I just know it was meant for you. What are the chances it would find its way to a small town like this otherwise? You say you haven't seen one just like the other one in all these years?"

"No, I haven't . . . and I've looked," Emily responded. "It's one of the few nice things we had. It always made my Christmases so special. But your tea. I came over here to warm your tea."

"Thank you," Margaret said as Emily returned with her steaming cup. "I think it will look just wonderful here. I think we did a great job."

They both stood by the window overlooking the Blue Ridge Mountains, the window being possibly the nicest feature of the chain motor hotel that had been converted into a reasonably priced retirement home in this small foothills town. Emily often wondered why a town this size had ever been envisioned to support a five-story hotel, but she was happy that someone had tried—and had failed. She didn't think there could have been a nicer place for her to retreat to in this time of her life.

The two women stood there and enjoyed their handiwork for several minutes. A small silver aluminum tree from the fifties reached up more than three feet at one end of the oak drop-leaf table

Emily's great-grandfather and wife had taken across the Appalachians in a wagon on their grand adventure into the West. Emily's own father had brought it back across the mountains, dismantled and in the trunk of his Hudson, generations later and stored it in the attic of their Virginia home on the banks of a lazy stream in a ravine coming down off Old Rag Mountain. It was the only thing from Emily's family that had been recovered after the rogue hurricane had turned the stream into a torrent in the middle of the night and collapsed the house on top of Emily's parents while she was away in her first year at the teacher's college.

Now the tree looked perfect on top of the table set off against the background of the snow-covered Blue Ridge. The rest of the top of the table was now spread with clouds of angel hair. Just waiting for the treasure that Emily had been saving for since she'd seen it in the window of Mulberry Junction a scant five weeks ago. Emily had actually been saving for it for several years, setting aside whatever she didn't need for personal expenses as well as the occasional shortfall monetary gift she didn't turn right around and spend on small notions for her nieces and nephews. Emily just hadn't realized what she'd been saving that money for until she'd walked by the window of Mulberry Junction as they were taking down their Halloween display and putting up their Christmas display.

"I guess I should be going," Margaret said, breaking the spell of their shared reverie. "You'll be wanting to go down into the town. The store will be closing early today."

"Yes, I guess it's time," Emily said, her voice choking from the excitement of making the purchase but edged with the fear that her bubble would burst and either the price hadn't been reduced enough yet or that someone else had snatched her treasure from her. "I'll let you know when I have it. And then I'd be pleased if you came up and spent Christmas Eve here with me. I've also asked Jessica. I know she'll be alone otherwise."

Margaret rolled her eyes, being careful that Emily didn't see her do so. She agreed that Jessica would probably normally be alone this Christmas. The residents here avoided her like the plague. She was loud, grasping, and self-centered—and she had a nasty knack of assessing the cost of anything anyone bought along with the embarrassing talent of usually being right on the money with her loudly announced estimate, which was most unwelcome in a community like this where everyone was living on the sharp edge of barely muddling through. But this was just like Emily. Always giving; never taking. That was why Margaret was so excited about this extravagance Emily was setting out to undertake. Emily needed something expensive and beautiful like this in her life.

* * * *

Emily almost couldn't bear to look at the luminous windows of Mulberry Junction in the distance as she walked down main street from the residence hall into the center of the small town. It was getting dark and another light snow had started. The holiday light display was modest, in keeping with the struggling economy of the town, but the duskiness of the late afternoon in early winter and the snowflakes helped make the atmosphere festive. Anticipation electrified the air. Emily could see it in how alive the town was with activity. And she could see it in the eyes of those passing her by, either en route to last-minute Christmas shopping or on their way home from the stores.

She couldn't help herself. She had to look for it in Mulberry Junction's window when she was still two blocks away. She couldn't see it, though. For a brief moment she was afraid it was gone, and her heart fluttered dangerously. But then she realized that she couldn't see into the window because a woman and child were standing there.

Ah, yes, it was still there, Emily realized as she drew closer. But her heart continued to flutter and she felt herself trembling with fear and anticipation. Her fear was dispelled as she drew close enough to see that the price had been knocked down to just within her spending capability. This only made her trembles of anticipation increase to take up the slack.

It was gorgeous. The figurines were larger than normal. They were made out of terra cotta and were painted, obviously by loving hand, in several luminous shades of brilliant colors—not completely covered, the terra cotta artfully showing through here and there, but in bright dabs of red, blue, green, purple, white, and silver—really silver that had been applied in molten form to the terra cotta. Emily knew this process had required precision. The silver had to be liquefied enough to accommodate the design, but not so hot as to burst the terra cotta base. Blue dominated for the figure of Mary, and purple for Joseph. The angel glowed with a bright white, and the Baby Jesus shown forth in a rich, deep red. Their faces and hands were designated in perfectly formed applications of silver. Other figures were there too, a whole complement of them—shepherds and kings and sheep and cows and camels and even the donkey that had brought the family to the large, unpainted terra cotta stable that framed the Holy Family.

The Italian crèche was beautiful in its own right, exuding a contrasting feeling of delicacy and strength, earthiness and wonder. but to Emily's eyes it was far more than that. It was as near identical as she could remember across the decades of the crèche that her mother had brought with her to her marriage, possibly her family's most precious possession—beyond each other. Emily's mother had brought it out on Christmas Eve every year when Emily was a young girl and they had put it under the Christmas tree. And it would be whisked away on Epiphany twelve days later. Its appearance and disappearance bracketed the Christmas season for Emily. She had particularly been drawn to the Baby Jesus in his golden splendor. And seeing the attraction for her daughter, Emily's mother had permitted her to lift this single figurine out of the crèche and stroke the cool terra cotta and murmur her secret delight to him as he blissfully slept away.

Emily's father had once remarked to his wife that she shouldn't let Emily handle the figurine like that for fear of rubbing the silver leaf away, but Emily had heard her mother respond that Jesus was meant to be shared and that she was just glad that Emily was drawn to him as she was.

The crèche had been swept away in the same flood that had taken the lives of Emily's parents, and memories of it had stayed fresh in Emily's mind, becoming something that she was searching for, some sense to be taken out of a hard life and from seemingly senseless tragedies such as life-taking floods.

Emily had eventually accepted that she wouldn't get the answers she sought out of life; she was just happy that she'd lived long and had been able to touch the lives of so many of her students.

And, yes, she was thankful that she had her small apartment in the retirement residence and good friends like Margaret when so many in the world, in this community even, had little or nothing.

Then the miracle. The crèche had come to her small town and had made itself available to her as a goal she could still attain in her life. And here it was. It was still here and in a few moments it would be hers. Her eyes sought the Baby Jesus. Yes, the same one—at least her memory fought to make it so—its golden paint perhaps even more luminous than her mother's figurine. New, probably unhandled by human touch.

Emily involuntarily reached out, wanting to touch the small figure in the manger, even though she knew it was behind glass. Her hand instead touched the matted glove of a child, a hand also reaching out and touching the glass just beyond the grasp of the Baby Jesus. Emily looked down, first at the glove, which was threadbare and had a hole in it here and there, and then at the face of the child. She was no more than six or seven, and her eyes were greedily drinking in the crèche. But not the whole sweep of the crèche; she was focused on the Baby Jesus.

"Come on, Rose, we have to be going," a young woman with a gaunt, haunted look to her and wrapped in a thin coat inadequate to the elements was whispering to the little girl. "We have to get back to give Ronny his medicine. You know we can't have that. We'll come back tomorrow to see it again, if you like. But we've got to go, Rose. The stove will be needing more logs. You know Ronny can't take cold."

"Just a few more minutes, please," the girl said in a sad, plaintive voice. "Look, he looks so peaceful, Mom. He looks like Ronny."

Emily turned away, embarrassed at having intruded in the family scene, even if not on purpose. She entered the store and stood by the front display until the clerk came forward.

As the clerk was taking the figurines out of the window and carefully wrapping them individually in tissue paper, Emily looked beyond the window. The woman was pulling the little girl away from the store, but the little girl was still turned to the window, her eyes glued to the Baby Jesus figurine. Tears streaming down her face.

* * * *

"How could she afford something like that?" Jessica was hissing under her breath to Margaret as Emily was bustling around her kitchenette putting out cups and saucers and opening a tin of cookies. "I saw a set just like it in the window at Mulberry Junction, and it was as dear as six months' worth of fees in this dump."

"Oh, I think it's been in the family for years," Margaret whispered back, doing her best to keep a serene smile plastered on her face.

"Humph," Jessica chortled. "That or on deep discount. It isn't even all there. It's missing the most important piece. There's no baby. Why does she even put it out, when there's no Jesus here."

"Oh, I think Jesus is here," Margaret said in secret delight. "Emily told me she had an opportunity to give the Jesus figure away to someone who needed it. She said something about Jesus not needing to be kept hidden away—needing to be shared."

"How . . . unusual," Jessica snorted, rolling her eyes at Margaret.

"Yes . . . unfortunately," Margaret whispered back, and then turned away so that Jessica couldn't see her mischievous smile.

# Clyde Saves Christmas

Christine and Clyde loved Anne and Jim Randall's house. It spread out on many levels and had all sorts of interesting rooms filled with a lifetime of treasures—although Jim called it Oriental junk—from years of residence in East Asia and the Middle East.

Christine was partial to the tall carved wooden pillar that had come off a Thai temple and that Jim referred to as his Thai toothpick. Whenever the Randalls weren't looking, Christine stretched up on this pillar and pretended to sharpen her front claws, claws that she could only pretend to sharpen, because the Randalls had had hers removed when she was just a kitten. But she was most enticed by the large pottery jars the Randalls had brought back from the Middle East and kept in their den. Christine had graduated from one cool, dark pot to the next larger one as she grew from a kitten into a refined middle-aged lady. She could spend most of a day curled up inside whatever pot currently fit her, dreaming of goldfish swirling around in a pond.

For his part, to Clyde, who was old enough to no longer be labeled as middle aged, the most intriguing treasures in the Randall's collection were the two rattan elephant side tables. The rattan sides of the tables were just right for sharpening the front claws he didn't have either. And the elephants' wooden tusks were perfect to scratch the itches Clyde couldn't get to with his hind claws, which he still had. Clyde was just as attracted to the big, cool earthenware pots as Christine was, but he rarely jumped in one, because he had found that his arthritis prevented him from jumping out of even the largest pot on his own anymore.

Christmas morning found Christine and Clyde in seventh heaven, staring down the twinkling colored lights and batting at low-slung balls on the tree and cavorting around the ribbons and wrapping paper Anne and Jim had strewn around on the floor of the den as they opened their presents and oohed and awed over the knick knacks that friends and family assumed they still were collecting for their overstuffed house.

Christine looked up suddenly at the strange sound coming from Anne and the tearing up of her mistress's eyes as Anne held up a delicate black necklace. Christine sniffed at it, discerning that it was made out of human hair, which she'd never known to compose any of those other fascinating, shiny things Anne wore around her neck and wrists and on her ears. Just human hair. That must be why Anne was so sad about the present, Christine reasoned. It wasn't shiny; it was just human hair—very old human hair at that. If she'd really been able to understand those noises humans made, of course, Christine would have known that the present had been a belatedly delivered legacy from Anne's Aunt Suzie, who had died two months earlier, and who had asked that Anne receive this family heirloom at Christmas time with the message that Aunt Suzie knew Anne would preserve and cherish it—and, in her own time, pass it on—as no one else in the family would.

But to Christine, the present had just made Anne sad—just as the bright gold cuff links Jim had just opened had made him scowl. Christine didn't need to translate the human noises to know why Jim was unhappy with this present. Ever since the Randalls and their Siamese cats had flown over the ocean from that exotic, tropical place Christine and Clyde had been born, Jim refused to wear anything that would require such shiny fasteners at his wrists. Christine knew Jim had had enough of that life, and she was just as happy that he spent most of his days now in the house, providing a lap and extra strokes. The shiny wrist fasteners frightened Christine somewhat. Did this mean Jim was going to be gone from the house more now? Was he going back to his old life? Would she be cooped up in that jostling cage in the belly of a big silver bird again? Christine hadn't liked that at all.

The Randalls moved to the breakfast room, leaving Christine and Clyde to roll around in the stray wrappings until Clyde got bored and Christine got tired.

Later in the day, Christine awoke to the sound of Anne frantically searching around in the den for something. Christine emerged from her pot and tried to help Anne look, although she had no idea what Anne was looking for, and Anne seemed to become even more frantic with Christine rubbing against her leg as she searched around the room. Earlier in the afternoon, Jim had cleared the wrapping paper out. He had marched off with it wadded up in his arms and was now burning it in the fireplace in the living room.

41

Anne walked quickly to the living room, with Christine right behind her, and started to make those quick, insistent noises that humans seemed to need to make to communicate with each other. Jim made the noises back at her, and they both looked toward the fireplace with the saddest expressions on their faces that Christine had ever seen the two make.

For the rest of the afternoon, Anne wandered listlessly around the house with tears in her eyes and Jim seemed to have disappeared beyond that door in the breakfast room that led to a cold room filled with a couple of big metal cans. At last, Anne settled in an arm chair in the den and stared at the Christmas tree, not really seeing it because of the tears that kept building up in her eyes. Christine hopped onto Anne's lap and let Anne stroke her. Christine knew that was the best medicine for whatever strange sickness Anne had.

Christine was the first one to hear the noise—a resonating, forlorn mewing that came from over by the Christmas tree. She knew instantly what the problem was, but it took Anne several minutes to even hear the noise let alone to take any action. Christine hopped off Anne's lap an instant before Anne realized where the noise was coming from and what it meant. Christine beat her mistress to her current favorite earthenware pot in time to see Clyde's muzzle appear briefly at the neck of the pot and then disappear as he slid back down to the bottom.

Clyde was stuck in Christine's pot. Oh, no, Christine thought. Now the jig was up. Anne and Jim would really be sad now.

Anne reached over and turned the pot on its side so that Clyde could scamper out of his prison. As she did so, the lights of the tree glittered off something in the pot. She reached in with her hand and pulled out several ribbons and a bow—and Jim's new cuff links and Aunt Suzie's hair necklace.

Christine tried to tell her mistress that she was sorry, that she had tried to take the sadness away that the necklace and cuff links had brought to Anne and Jim earlier, but, to her great surprise and disgust, Anne was laughing and squealing and hugging both Christine and Clyde and running off toward that door in the breakfast room in search of Jim, Clyde in full dash behind her.

Humans, Christine thought. They were so unpredictable and frustrating. She briefly sat and groomed herself for a few minutes, and then she picked up the ribbons and bow that Anne had left behind and retreated with them to her pot to dream of goldfish twirling around in a pond.

# A Monterey Christmas

"Look at that sun shine. Another beautiful Monterey morning."

Yes, it certainly was, the boy thought. His face set in such a grim line that his father gave him a perplexed look. The weather report the previous night had talked about a cold snap, and the boy had bounced out of bed early this morning and rushed to the door, so sure that, although almost too late, the white Christmas he had known in their Colorado valley had finally reached them on the California coast.

"No snow." The statement was curt and tense; the words clipped.

"Of course not, silly," said his dad. "It's cooler than yesterday, but it's still a balmy 70 degrees." Dad took a deep breath and smiled up at the sky. "Have you ever seen such a glorious day?"

Obviously the boy had. He sank down on the step up to the front porch and buried his chin in his fists. His dad just didn't understand. The snow was just a symbol of everything gone wrong.

At last Dad caught on, and he sat down on the step beside his son. "Listen, big guy, you know we moved here because we

44

learned those Colorado winters were bad for your condition. Christmas comes to California just like it comes to Colorado, you know."

The boy moved ever so slightly away from his dad. "Does not; in Colorado it comes with snow."

A long pause. Dad nudged his son playfully with an elbow, but the boy wasn't having any of that today. With a audible sigh, Dad stood up. "Well, times a wastin', and we have things to do." He yelled back toward the open front door, "Mom, need some soap flakes, matches, and food coloring. Think you can rustle those up for us?"

The boy knew his dad was just trying to catch his attention, and he sank his chin deeper into his hands and hunched his shoulders. Life was the pits. Nothing had been right since they moved here.

Dad moved toward the door. "Well, you gonna' come in and help?"

A long pause. "Can't. Told Jimmy I'd bike over to his place this morning."

Dad gave him a sharp look and almost said something. But then he just shrugged his shoulders and walked into the house.

The boy's mood only darkened further when he arrived at Jimmy's. Jimmy and his mom were bustling around, packing suitcases, and chattering with excitement. A happy family.

"What's up?" the boy asked.

"Mom and I are going up into the mountains for Christmas," Jimmy answered. His eyes were dancing with joy.

Up into the mountains. Snow. The boy couldn't help it. Tears formed in his eyes. He was so homesick for his Colorado mountain valley and the life he'd left behind.

"That's . . . that's great," he finally managed to get out. "Your dad going too?"

"Naw," Jimmy responded with a slight frown. "He says he don't like the cold and snow and has a golfin' game to go to here on Christmas Eve. He and Mom aren't talkin' . . . again."

"Oh, that's too bad," the boy said. But what was really too bad was that Jimmy was going to get to go to the mountains and have a white Christmas and he wasn't. And suddenly that was just too much to bear. He jumped back on his bicycle and managed a "Have a great time" before he wheeled off. But he couldn't help finishing it off with, "I sure wish it was me."

Jimmy watched his friend pump off down the street. He had seen the tears and heard the hurt. He looked up at his mother, and she knew what he was going to ask even before he opened his mouth.

The boy was fighting the bile of resentment as he reached home, but he was losing that battle. Jimmy was his best friend, but why did Jimmy have all the luck? Why did Jimmy's parents love him so much that he could go to snow for Christmas? Why had everyone else gotten all of the good parents who understood and did something about it?

As he entered the house, he heard his dad off in the dining room. He was whistling the "White Christmas" song, and the boy almost burst into tears on the spot. The music drew him to the dining room, however, and there were his dad and mother—and something the boy had never seen before.

Dad had taken down the big mirror over the buffet and had it leaning up against some boxes on the dining room table. Mom was standing in the doorway to the kitchen, pouring Ivory Snow flakes into a bowl and whipping up what must have been a second or third batch of fluffy white soap suds. They foamed up to look just like . . . snow.

Dad had just about finished making a picture on the mirror. When he saw the boy enter the room, he gathered him in with an arm and started pointing out the features of the Christmas mural he had created. The mountains that had been made out of white soap suds enclosed a miniature valley with log houses made out of matchsticks, pine trees made with dyed soap suds, and an area left open to the mirror surface that looked just like a frozen lake. One matchstick man was skiing down a mountain and another was skating on the pond.

The boy gasped in recognition. This looked just like their Colorado mountain valley at Christmas time. The picture was beautiful. He never knew his dad could make something so beautiful. And he had done it just for him.

Mom, Dad, and the boy sat around the dining room table, murmuring to each other and laughing at the occasional joke as Dad put the finishing touches on the Christmas picture. The phone rang, and Mom told the boy it was for him.

"Hi, this is Jimmy. My mom wants to know if you want to go to the mountains with us this Christmas. Can you? I know it would be fun."

The boy was nearly speechless. "Uh, thanks Jimmy. I mean .
. . really thanks. That would be wonderful . . . and I really, really
appreciate you asking . . . but my dad has asked me to help him with
something tomorrow, and I really gotta stay here and do it."

The next day, Jimmy and his mom waved from their car as
they passed the house on their way to the mountains. The boy and
his parents waved back enthusiastically and then returned to
spreading whipped Ivory Snow soapsuds into the shape of
snowflakes and drifting snow on the front windows of their
bungalow under the warm Monterey sun.

# Gifts

"Tell me again, Raul. Tell me about your tree."

I sighed, smoothed out the wrinkles of the blanket covering Hosea's legs, and started the story again. Hosea's eyes twinkled and his smile told me that his interest in the story was blocking out the pain. That in itself would have been enough for me to repeat the story, but the story still excited me too, so I didn't mind saying it all again.

"Can you see it over there in the corner, Hosea?" I asked. "Can you see it standing tall, all the way to the ceiling, with lights, and bright, shiny ornaments—and with the angel Gabriel high on top, trumpeting the good news?"

"Yes, yes, I can see it, Raul," Hosea said, as he clapped his hands in delight. My friend was peering intently into the dark corner of his shabby little room, and the brightness of his delight made the gloom and squalor of the sick room disappear. "Tell me again, Raul. Tell me about how you will get such a wonderful Christmas tree."

"It has been our project all year, Hosea," I answered, spinning a story that Hosea had already heard three times during this visit. "I asked my parents if we could have a real Christmas tree this year, with lights and everything. I said that I just knew if we all worked hard all year, and put aside a little bit each week from all our jobs, we could have such a tree this year. We already have a Christmas tree, of course, but it is a short, false tree, with tired, fading paper leaves, that Papa has pulled out of a cardboard tube and fluffed out every year since before I was born. We can't put lights on it, Papa said—if we had any lights to put on it, of course—or it would burn our apartment house down. And its branches have become too weak even to hold up those paper ornaments we made for it two years ago. So, last year I asked Papa and Mama if, for this year, we could have a new tree, a real tree, with lights and everything. And with the angel Gabriel on top."

"And what did they say, Raul? What did your Papa answer?"

"My papa's face turned very serious and sad, and he said to me, 'Ah, but we are too poor, Raul. Everyone here is too poor. No one has money for such a tree, son.'"

Hosea sat up in his cot and leaned forward. I knew we had gotten to his favorite part of the story. "But what was your mama's answer to that, Raul? Tell me again what she said." He knew what my mama had said. I'm sure Hosea could say it with the same words I had used three times already today. And, indeed, I could see him mouthing the words as I retold what my mama had said.

I turned to Hosea and put my forehead against his and repeated slowly, so he could savor every word. "'You are right, Papa, of course,' my mama said, 'but we are only poor in our living; we aren't poor in our spirit. If we become poor in our spirit, we might as well stop living. Raul has given us a goal we can work for this year, a goal that will help us keep our spirits up. Let's do it, Papa. Let's see if we can have a real Christmas tree next year."

Hosea gave a contented little sigh and laid back down in his bed. He cast a dreamy look over toward the corner as if he could see our tree of the spirit. "All mamas must be the same," he said in a faraway voice. "My mama says that I must keep up my spirit too and that I must keep my eye on the goal of getting better."

I thought Hosea might be drifting off to sleep, but he suddenly sat up on his cot, opened the drawer of the little stand next to his bed, and gazed intently inside. I knew this was where he kept his toy soldiers, the favorite of his few toys, which had fed his imagination and filled his time for many weeks now. He took three of the little paint-chipped metal figures out of the drawer and examined each one, in turn, closely. Finally, he handed the one with the brightest paint to me and, in an excited voice, said, "Here, Raul, when you have your tree, could you put this on it so that I can share my Christmas with you?"

"But, Hosea, I said, I don't have my tree yet; we haven't even found out if we've really earned enough money. I just tell my story like it's really going to happen so that I won't lose hope. And this is your best soldier. I think—"

"Oh, please, please take it and put it on your tree," Hosea said, as he took my hand and folded my fingers over the toy soldier. "I know you'll have your tree. Your mama said so. And I want something of mine to be on your tree. Now," he said as he laid his head back down on the cot, clearly exhausted from the effort of finding and bestowing his gift, "tell me the rest of the story. Tell me of your plan for getting your Christmas tree and what you have done."

I looked over into the corner where Hosea had envisioned my tree both so that Hosea wouldn't see the tears in my eyes and to gain strength from what he had seen there. But all I could see was the crumbling plaster and the dimness of the late-afternoon's waning light. I sighed and picked up the story again. "We all decided, my papa, my mama, and I, that we'd do a little extra work every week, all year long, and that we'd put the extra money from that in the little tin box on the shelf in the kitchen. We wouldn't open the tin box until just before Christmas. I asked for a few more streets to be added to my paper route and got the doctor to let me help groom his daughter's horse, and I said my goal would be to buy the tree. Papa worked extra hours at the factory, and he said he'd buy the lights. Mama took in a bit more laundry and said she wanted to pay for some ornaments. If there was enough money left over, we'd buy that figure of the angel Gabriel I'd seen in the shop near the church. Tonight is the night when we find out—"

I had turned to face Hosea when I finished the story and found that he'd drifted off to sleep.

I tried to be cheerful with Hosea's mama when she asked me into the kitchen as I was leaving and offered me some fresh pineapple and a bit of cake. She thanked me for visiting with Hosea and said that she at least could offer me something sweet. I told her how much Hosea loved my story about the Christmas tree we were working to have, and although I knew what the answer would be, I asked her if there would be a tree for Hosea too.

"Oh dear me, no," Hosea's mama said. "We don't have time for that in this house." There was a pause, and then she said, "Everything I have is going into making Hosea well. Hosea is my Christmas. I was so afraid Hosea wouldn't be here to see Christmas, but Christmas is just two days away, and Hosea is holding his own. That's all Hosea and I can hope for."

"Well," I asked timidly, "Could Hosea come to my apartment on Christmas Day and see our Christmas tree—if we manage to get one?"

"Oh, no, I'm sorry, Raul," Hosea's mama said. "Hosea isn't well enough to leave his room." She turned her face to the wall, and I finished my cake and left after whispering my good-byes and my Christmas wishes for her and Hosea.

That evening, Papa gathered Mama and me around the kitchen table and, with much ceremony, opened the tin box. Papa hummed a Christmas song and Mama laughed and clapped her hands as coins spilled out onto the kitchen table. Both noticed that I wasn't being happy too, though, and Papa spoke to me in his serious voice. "What is the matter, Raul?" he asked. "Are you afraid there isn't enough money for our Christmas tree?"

"No, Papa," I answered, and then I started to cry and told him what was bothering me.

On Christmas morning, we all came into our living area after Mama had lit some candles around the room. The presents under the tree weren't many, but the wrappings were bright and cheerful and seemed to glow in the candlelight. Mama's old paper tree didn't look so bad in the dancing light, either, and the little toy soldier Papa had managed to fasten to its top gave it a dignified air.

Mama had set hot cocoa out for us, and we had barely been able to take a sip when we heard a knock. Mama answered the door, and Hosea's mama came bustling in. She was crying as she hugged Mama, Papa, and me in turn.

"I came because Hosea asked me to," she said when she had finished making the rounds. "I did as you asked. I told him nothing. But as soon as he woke and saw that Christmas tree all lit up in the corner of his room, he asked me to come straight here. He said he knew that Raul would have a wonderful tree of his own, but he would be very pleased if your whole family could come over and share *his* Christmas tree with him. And Hosea wanted me to be sure to tell Raul that Gabriel was trumpeting the good news on top of his tree too."

# What to Do with Rusty

Aunt Peg's brush with being gassed couldn't have happened at a more inopportune time. Angela had just finished the paperwork on her retirement from the Foreign Service and was still waiting for the movers to arrive at her new house when she was called to come get Peg's cat, Rusty, and take it to the vet's while Peg was hauled off to the emergency room to have her lungs checked. Peg had turned on the stove in her condo with the pilot light out and had been roused hours latter by her old, half-lame cat as she was drifting away. She'd had the presence of mind to throw open all of the doors and windows and get the gas off before tragedy had resulted, so little was actually said—at least to her face—about the state of her faculties. Peg didn't mind going, especially by just drifting off to sleep, but she was mortified at the thought of what might have happened to the others in her apartment building in the process—not the least her beloved Rusty.

Angela had known she, as the only relative living nearby, was going to have to face the struggle of Peg giving up her independence and moving into a home sooner or later, but it had been quite inconvenient to have it slap her in the face just now.

Angela had just purchased her first home, thanks to a large gift of money from Aunt Peg when she had moved out of her house into a condo. She had gotten a fairly large house, because she had accumulated considerable porcelain and crystal during her years in Europe—added to what she had been given by Aunt Peg when she had downsized—and Peg's incident with the gas stove had come just while Angela was trying to get settled.

It had been a hard move and transition for Angela. The Foreign Service had been her entire life and had kept her so busy she hadn't developed any outside interests. Now, she was back in the States, completely isolated from the life she had known, and with nothing to do other than perfect her new house.

The up side of the situation was that Aunt Peg didn't have to be convinced it was time to let someone else care for her; the down side was that Angela just didn't have time to face this now. But that didn't really prove to be the down side. The gas stove incident had occurred just after Halloween, and Aunt Peg found a home she liked before Thanksgiving, but now Rusty had become the stumbling block. Try as either Aunt Peg or Angela might, neither had been able to find an appropriate home for an aging, fat, long-haired cat with a droopy disposition and a lame leg. Aunt Peg had had Rusty since before her husband had died, and she couldn't bear to place him with just anybody. Truth be known, she could barely face parting with him at all. He had been the only family she'd had close to her for the last decade.

So, it was the middle of December already and, in frustration and with far more feigned willingness than Angela wanted to admit, she had agreed for Aunt Peg to bring Rusty over to her new house for a visit to see if Angela could possibly be able to take the cat in.

That was what had brought us to this crucial day. Aunt Peg bustled into Angela's living room and perched in a rocking chair right next to the Christmas tree that was decorated with delicate crystal ornaments Angela had picked up around Europe over a good many years. This was the first time she'd been able to put them all on display at one time.

Rusty huddled trembling in Aunt Peg's lap, knowing that something significant was afoot, but also knowing he would not be happy about what that might be.

Aunt Peg was a nervous wreck. She knew this was Rusty's last chance at a home where she might still be able to visit him from time to time. She was trying her best to show him off to good effect in front of Angela, but she was failing miserably, and Rusty wasn't helping at all. He just buried his face into the bosom of her dress and hissed at Angela whenever she came near. After an initial stilted conversation, Angela excused herself to put the tea on in the kitchen. She had just lifted one her favorite porcelain tea pots down from the shelf on which it was displayed with a good many others like it, when she heard the sound of shattering glass from the living room. The unexpected sound made her drop her tea pot into the kitchen sink, where it shattered into six different pieces.

Tears bubbled up into Angela's eyes, as she rushed back into the living room. There, she found several of the crystal ornaments from the tree on the floor and the tree still swaying a bit, as Rusty hopped back into Aunt Peg's lap and buried his muff into an opening in her cardigan sweater.

Aunt Peg was speechless, just staring at Angela in misery as she entered the room. Angela bubbled over with rage and hurt, and she knew that she would lash out at her Aunt if she were forced to say anything at all at this point. All of this work to get her house just right and all of these beautiful things she had accumulated, and they were shattering around her because of some old cat that should just be put down.

Angela mumbled something that couldn't really be interpreted to mean anything at all, and, fetching a broom and dustpan, quickly swept up the broken crystal and marched back toward the kitchen.

"Oh, I'm so sorry," Aunt Peg finally managed to say to her niece's back. "And what was that I heard from the kitchen? Something else broken?"

The question just hung in the air. Angela was already through the door into the kitchen, letting it swing shut behind her. She made a brutal jab at the trash can with the dustpan and emptied possibly $200 of once fine, but now worthless, glass into the trash. Then she marched over to the sink, gathered up the porcelain shards and threw them away as well.

She stood at the sink, gripping the edge with her hands, her knuckles turning white. She slowly counted down from fifty, regulating her breath with her counting. The radio was playing, and she concentrated on the words of "The Little Drummer Boy" while fighting for control. It very likely was the first time she'd ever concentrated on those words: "The finest gifts we bring . . . to lay before our king."

She now felt calm enough to resume making a pot of tea. She reached up for a replacement tea pot for the one that had broken and, for the first time, realized just how many porcelain tea pots she had. She counted them slowly. She had nine porcelain tea pots, not counting the broken one. For some reason, this made Angela giddy, and she started to laugh. It took her more than a minute to regain control of herself, and then she made the tea and opened the cupboard to find tea cups. She saw that she had tea cups by the dozens. She had tea cups to go with each of those porcelain tea pots. She found the ones that went with the tea pot she was using and arranged these and a sugar bowl and some cookies on one of several trays she found in the cupboard under the sink.

As she was arranging the tray, Angela recalled the look her aunt had given her when she'd entered the living room to view the broken crystal. It had been a look of fear and despair and of defeat. And Angela remembered how that old, lame cat—the cat that had been her aunt's sole companion for over a decade and that had pawed at his mistress to get her attention as her condo was filling with gas—had retreated to Aunt Peg's lap and how Aunt Peg had sheltered him, desperately hugging him to her in her despair.

Angela stopped fussing with the tray and steeled herself for what she had to do next. She counted to twenty this time until her nerves had calmed. Then, she picked up the tray and marched back into the living room.

Aunt Peg still had that miserable look on her face, as Angela put the tray down on the coffee table and sat down in a chair closely facing her aunt.

"Angela, I know . . ."

"Aunt Peg, I can't take your cat."

"I know, my dear. I'm so sorry. All these beautiful things. I know you can't have a cat like Rusty here." She was so close to tears she could barely get the words out. "But I've tried everything I can think of. I just wished they'd let me have him at the home. I guess there's nothing else to do. I'll just have to have him—"

"Oh, shush, Aunt Peg. Don't even say it. I mean that I can't take your cat from you at all. I can see what you mean to each other. I'll take Rusty, but only if you'll come with him. There's plenty of room here. I don't have to have all of this stuff out where the cat will stumble over it. I'm lonely too and haven't any notion of what to do with my life now. You've asked me several times what I want for Christmas. I've never answered, because I already have too much of everything in this house. But what I don't have in this house is a family. Can I have you and Rusty as my family as a present for my first Christmas here?"

# How Big the Ocean

"Just don't—"

"Screw it up again?" I nearly yelled into the cell phone. I wasn't angry; it was just hard to talk over the crying in the backseat. I actually laughed.

"I didn't mean that," Helen answered in a wounded voice. "It's just that you can be so . . . so . . ."

"Flighty?" I offered, accompanied by a snort. I turned my head and told the two girls back there to pipe down, but that had no effect at all. You can't reason with a Siamese cat being subjected to something it didn't choose.

"Sandra!" Helen said. I always knew when she'd had enough. She called me Sandra rather than Sandi.

"I'm just kidding you," I responded. "I know you've pulled strings—yet again—to get me this job interview. I think the world of you for doing this, and I promise I'll get there on time . . . if I can."

"S-a-n-d-r-a . . . are those children I hear crying in the background? Have you gone off track again?"

"Sorry, hon, gotta go. I think my exit is coming up." I shut down the phone and argued with myself on whether this was the exit for the Siamese rescue center. It was, but I hadn't decided that in time, and now I'd have to go to the next exit and turn back. And I was already running late for getting to that interview. Darn!

It was great that Helen had gotten me this interview. She'd always been the steady one. We'd been inseparable through seminary, where we were both preparing to be ministers of education, but then Helen had gone steadily up, and I'd had to row double time just to stay on the surface of the water. "You'll never make it anywhere, if you don't apply yourself and find good jobs in churches," Helen had constantly said. And she was right, I hadn't gone anywhere.

Helen had moved up quickly in her jobs—saved souls and gathered accolades. And I had yet to be placed in a church job at all. I was a failure as a Christian. My mother had been diagnosed with Alzheimer's right when I was being anointed, and as hard as Helen had tried to get me into church positions since my mother passed, I was still on the outside looking in.

Helen would have had a fit if she'd known that I had agreed to get these cats to the Siamese rescue center on my way to this job interview Helen had gotten for me in a big church in a university town. But the center was on my way—well, not more than fifty miles out of the way—and we were coming on to Christmas. This was high season for placing cats in homes. These little girls in the backseat needed every opportunity possible to find a home by Christmas.

As it turned out, either my maps weren't too helpful or I was busy cajoling the cats when I should have been looking at the road, because it took far too long to find the rescue center, and then

I had to move my old rattletrap beyond its endurance to make the university town in time. I headed for the center of town, knowing the church was near there, and after circling around for a while, I found, by driving right up to the edge of it and running out of road, that they had bricked over their main street to make a nifty walking mall.

I never asked, but Shantay must have really thought I was a sight when she came upon me as I sat there in my dusty Civic, watching the minutes between where I was and where I needed to be fritter away, where the asphalt was divided from red brick by a couple of metal barriers. I was looking bewilderedly at the flickering fairy lights in the trees on the pedestrian mall in the waning light of day when Shantay hefted her ample bosoms on the passenger windowsill and scrunched her ebony face down to where she could look me in the eye. Her hair radiated in gray and black wisps from a wrinkled, expressive face that managed to display humor and slight concern simultaneously.

Sensing her presence, I looked up into the face of a woman who looked just about as far down on her luck as possible, and every good intention I had of making that job interview in seven more minutes was shattered when she put on a sympathetic expression and said, "You all right, honey? Do you need help?"

She was asking me if *I* needed help.

Shantay—who had been quick to tell me that was her name—was wheezing so hard when she asked this that I was bewildered at how she could help me. From what I could see, the only reason she was half standing was because she was propped against the side of my car. And yet she seemed to be genuinely concerned about me.

I told her what church I was looking for, and she wrinkled up her nose but did turn and point up the hill behind me—where the church quite obviously was perched.

"Thanks," I said. "But why the hesitancy?"

"Not my first choice of churches," Shantay answered through hard breathing. "I used to sleep up there under their portico, but then they put in steel grates to keep us from doin' that. Usually sleep over by the library now. There's room over there, if—"

"No thanks," I answered. "I have a room reserved for the night. In fact—"

It was an instantaneous decision, one of those flighty acts of mine that always sent Helen into mumbling and grumbling. But it was getting dark, and I suddenly wasn't so sure I wanted to work at that church anyway.

It was getting to where it was decidedly cool at night even here in the South—we were entering the Christmas season, and Shantay was looking pretty delicate despite her massive bulk. So I told her I'd love to share her graciously offered space with her, but I already had two rooms reserved down at the Days Inn, and I couldn't see why either of them should go to waste, so why didn't she take one of those rooms for the night and, if she would, perhaps she could come to dinner with me—that I really hated to eat alone.

Shantay said nothing when I went into the motel office, praying all the way that they had two rooms available, which they did. I got the impression while we ate that evening at the Red Lobster restaurant attached to the motel that it had been some time since Shantay had gotten a good meal. She was a real Christmas gift to me. She was a great conversationalist and could conjure up a basic truth faster and clearer than anyone who had taught me at the seminary. She was always ready to laugh even when she knew it would finish off in a painful cough—a cough I had heard too often before and knew where that would lead too soon. I wished that everyone could face the inevitable as well as Shantay was doing.

We got into talking about Christmas and Christmas gifts, and I asked her what she had always wanted and never gotten. She sat and thought and chewed and coughed for a long minute.

"Well, you know, I've had about everything I needed in life. But if I had a choice of a Christmas present, I do believe I'd ask to see the ocean. I've never seen that and I'm told it's just over yonder. And I'm told it's pretty big. Yes, I think I'd like to see the ocean before I die."

I didn't like the look she gave when the subject of death came up, so I quickly said that I had never seen the Atlantic myself and had, in fact, left the Midwest with the intention of seeing the eastern shore and was just then on my way to getting that done.

Toward late afternoon of the next day, Shantay and I pulled up next to the sand at the poorer end of Virginia Beach. Shantay was a lot weaker by then than she had been the previous day, and I now understood why I had thrown that wheelchair into the trunk of the Civic back in Indianapolis after looking after Mrs. Bates to the end rather than leaving it behind as the neighbors had suggested.

As I wheeled Shantay out onto the sand as far as the wheelchair could go, she was giving off little clucking sounds and an occasional "Oh, my." It eventually got dark enough that we could barely see the water, but still Shantay sat there and stared out to sea. After a long stretch of silence, she gave a larger sigh than normal, trailing off into a disturbing cough, and allowed as how it was a very nice ocean but not quite as big as she had thought it would be. The deep smile lines on her face, however, belied any disappointment she might have expressed.

I was able to find a small rundown cottage just off the beach that, along with a few others, rented by the day. Shantay died three days later, but we had managed to get out on the sand every one of those days.

I called Helen to tell her I was sorry I had missed the job interview but something had come up and I hadn't made it there.

Helen wasn't too pleased at first. She said she knew I'd missed the appointment, because she'd talked to the minister at the church. She lit into me something fierce—the usual declarations of how I was just floating around and wasting my life on minutia and had wasted all that training to be a minister to people and how it was impossible to understand how the two of us could have turned out so different.

In the end, though, she sighed and said, "Reverend Claxton said they'd hold the interviews open if you could make it in the next day or two. I told him how good you'd be in the job—and that's the truth, Sandy. You'd be such an inspiration and a rock for people to cling to if you'd just settle down and apply yourself. And the reverend said he could hold off on a decision for two days. So, could you—?"

"I'll do what I can to be there, Helen. And again, thanks for trying to help me." I felt myself tearing up when I clicked off. Helen was such a good soul, and she was trying so hard with me. I knew I was a major disappointment to her. I just couldn't help myself.

It took all of the next day to make final arrangements for Shantay. While I was packing to leave, I heard one real corker of a domestic fight going on in the cottage next to ours. I can't say I was surprised. The young couple and their two toddlers had been in the cottage when we arrived, and they obviously had not been having a pleasant vacation. The man was a drinker, and the woman had skittered around like a frightened rabbit for days trying to keep the kids quiet and out of his way. But even when she had taken them out on the sand and settled them into making sandcastles, he would weave his way out there, scream at her about something that hadn't been done right, and set both kids off before returning to the cottage, jumping into his Camaro, and roaring off until late in the night.

When I carried my bag out to the Civic to leave for that interview in the university town church, his Camaro was kicking up dust once more, and it was loaded down so heavy I could tell the man didn't intend to come back. I was just closing the trunk when the woman staggered out of her cottage and collapsed into a weeping heap on the steps. She looked beat up pretty bad.

As I walked over toward her, all I could think of was that I wasn't going to be making it to that interview in time. In spite of all the good intentions in the world, I had once again proven to be a big disappointment to Helen.

# Bill-'N-Bob

Bill and Bob were virtually inseparable right up until good luck struck. The two had been unlikely best friends since Howard High. Bill's sandy hair; tall, thin stature; and love for making bets on everything imaginable was offset by Bob's dark, close-to-the-ground, pudgy appearance and puritanical pursing of lips whenever Bill launched into an "I'll bet you . . ." Of course, Bob never let Bill finish that sentence in his presence, but Bill never held it against him.

The two suffered the good-natured Mutt and Jeff comparisons of their classmates with bright smiles, and neither showed ire when they were jointly elected "Most Likely to Become Siamese Twins" at the end of their senior year. While others in their class wandered away from town to join the service or enroll in college, Bill and Bob took their own shared path. They even married, in a joint ceremony, two girls who were so much alike they could have held down the ends of a Broadway chorus line.

They became a fixture on the small town's Main Street, walking to work side by side in the morning, each in his starched white coat, and taking their lunches together either on the old bench outside the shop on warm days or over at Katie's luncheonette. In the evening, they strolled home side by side, Bill to 102 Elm Street and Bob to 104, while they reminisced on the day's head count.

Thanks to them, over the years Warner's Barber Shop became "the place to go" to get your ears lowered. The two cut hair at adjacent chairs and, together, put on a show that amazed and amused all of the men of the town—and a good number of the short-haired women as well. The two were always in a good mood and never took long to learn their clients' names and the locations of their funny bones. From morning to night, Bill and Bob maintained a running tag-team comedy show in which Bill never started a joke or sentence and Bob never ended one. The two became such a town institution that the local newspaper declared in its Fourth of July editorial that contentment within the community was embodied in the word "Bill-'N-Bob."

Then one day in running up to Christmas disaster made its appearance. Bob didn't even know that Bill was still following his vice—indeed there didn't seem to be an opportunity to do so, because the two were always so in step with each other. But that day right after Thanksgiving Bill won the state lottery. Bigtime. And it went right to his head.

The very morning Bill got the word tragedy struck. He draped his white coat from the mayor's upturned nose as the two crossed paths at the barber shop door, and leaving the Tuggle boy with half a crew cut and without so much as a word of good-bye to Bob, Bill was gone. Bob's lunch sack, the contents untouched, dragged mournfully near the ground as he trudged back to 104 Elm Street that evening. He arrived just in time to see the moving van back out of the driveway of 102 Elm, leaving nothing more than a stripped down Christmas tree in the corner of the living room.

Bill and his wife had, in fact, remembered to write a note to their neighbors before they left, announcing they were moving over to Winslow Estates right after they returned from a New Year's cruise—and they even included the adjoining-cabin cruise tickets they had obtained for Bob and his wife. But in the chaos they had forgotten to take the note next door, and it had been left on the kitchen counter in the now-empty house.

Bill and his wife had been surprised and a little more than hurt when Bob and his wife failed to show up for the cruise. Bill remembered Bob's attitude toward gambling and chalked Bob's snub up to jealousy and a mean streak Bill had never seen before.

More than once after they had returned to the town and had taken up residence in Winslow Estates, Bill's wife thought about inviting Bob and his wife to one of their barbecues, but she just never carried through. She knew that Bob and his wife just wouldn't be comfortable with their new set of friends. Truth be known, it was becoming increasingly harder to make *Bill* comfortable with their new set of friends. He was walking around in a blue funk most of the time and buying every new toy in sight to fill in the time.

For Bob and his wife's part, they quite clearly knew how it was when people—no matter how well you thought you knew them—suddenly got rich and decided they were too good for you. *They* certainly wouldn't embarrass themselves by calling Bill and his wife.

Months dragged into the summer, and Bob's despondency had turned into a petulance that wasn't at all good for business at

Warner's Barber Shop. There even was some talk of letting him go because his attitude was scaring what had once been faithful customers away. Business had become so slow that Bill's chair had been left vacant. This didn't help matters at all. During the early months following Bill's departure, Bob would get so busy that he forgot and would start up one of his jokes. He'd stop in mid joke and there would be a prolonged silence. Bob would have to look over at Bill's chair, only to remember that Bill wasn't there to finish the joke. Now Bob no longer looked at Bill's chair; he just gave a heavy sigh from time to time during what was becoming an increasingly sporadic appearance of a variety of heads that needed to be cut. Bob didn't even look too closely at the heads anymore. He just sighed and clipped—and sometimes apologized halfheartedly when ears were nipped from inattention.

Thus it was that one day Bob found what seemed to be a familiar head in his chair. At first he didn't pay it any mind, but it increasingly dawned on him that this man had a little gray streak right where Bill had one and that that pesky cowlick was just the same as Bill's. Just before it hit him that this *was* Bill's head in his chair, his former friend said in a pretty bad attempt at an English gentleman's accent, "Well, if you will not be so kind as to start a joke, how can you expect me to finish it?"

The barbershop erupted in laughter, and Bob turned beet red. Of all the humiliation. Not only had he been dumped by someone he had counted as his best friend, but now Bill had the gall to come in here and treat him like the downstairs maid. And everyone was laughing at him.

This time it was Bob's turn to rip off his coat and head for the door—this time the one at the back of the shop—leaving in his wake a bewildered mayor who had just been called to one of the other chairs and who once again found himself stumbling around and trying to pull a starched white jacket off his head.

The head barber was just two steps behind Bob as he exploded into the break room at the rear of the shop.

"Hey, Bob. Wait up. Whatcha do that for?"

"They laughed. *You* laughed, too. I guess you think it's real funny to see that two-faced gambler lording it over me. He ain't rich because he's better than me—or anyone else. He's rich because he showed up at a gas station window at the right time to buy a winning ticket."

"Now hold on, Bob. Bill wasn't making fun of you. He was trying to make up with you."

"Bull."

"No, not Bull. Bill. Your friend, Bill. What do you think he was doing in here today?"

"Isn't it obvious? He came in here just to make fun of me."

"Wrong. You are so wrong, Bob. He came in here today to ask me for his old job back. He found that being rich and hobnobbing with those folks over in Winslow Estates wasn't half as good as the life he'd left behind. He said he wanted his old chair back—the one right next to yours."

Silence.

"I ain't playing with you, Bob. Those were his very words. He just sat in your chair to start the good times rolling again."

Bob was out of the break room in a flash. He looked wildly around the shop but couldn't see Bill anywhere. The mayor smiled wanly and pointed to the door.

Bob saw Bill hunched over on the bench in the park. He knew it was him because of that gray streak and the cowlick with a mind of its own. He sat down next to his old friend and tried to think of something to say.

"You know, Bill . . ."

Bill, as of old, broke in, ". . . that it's going to be awful hard for me to go to the dance tonight with this half-done cut. Everyone's gonna want to know what barber did this to me."

"Well, come on back to the shop, then, and I'll finish the job."

"Can't do that. Something else I need to do first."

"What's that? Go on another cruise?"

"Nope. I'm not going to let you finish my hair until I've done yours—and showed you how a real barber works. Oh, and Bob?"

"What?"

"Has anyone moved into 102 yet?"

"Nope."

"Good."

# Betty's Birds

Connie felt the little tug at the back of her mind that it might have been weeks, months, or even years since she'd thought about how or what Betty Stapleton from next door was doing. This surprising thought occurred when, as she was about to bid three no trump, her partner, Amy Gaines, pointed toward Betty's back yard beyond Connie's glass family room doors. There an unusually large flock of red birds, cardinals, Connie assumed, were furiously kicking up the first week of the new year snow around a large bird feeder. With the mature boxwood and azalea hedges between the yards, the bridge foursome could only see the top two-thirds of the iron stake that suspended the feeder.

"Betty's birds," was what Connie first said in a chirpy voice, which caused a twittering of laughter around the bridge table. Crazy Betty and her love for birds and fixation on feeding them, especially through the winter months, had been the talk of the neighborhood for decades.

Connie had no idea why she was thinking of crazy Betty after all this time and in the middle of a bridge game, but she found her mind flipping through the years. She and the reclusive, quirky

Betty could not have been more different; Betty was even a generation older than she was. They had started off close enough as neighbors but primarily through their husbands and because Betty had taken care of Connie and her husband's kids and pets frequently as Connie accompanied her husband on far-flung business trips. Connie had been highly visible and highly successful—president of this and that and active on the state level of the Junior League. Conversely, dowdy old Betty, who had no children of her own, had stuck to her house and her birds—except for when she sat across the street with Mrs. Twilling between the time she fell and broke her hip and they found a home for her, or when she was out with Meals on Wheels, or when she helped that neighbor down the street with his kids for several years after his wife died so young. They even went to the same church, where Connie did important work—putting together all those Christmas pageants and church socials and chairing the altar guild, while Betty just sat in the nursery, worked in the weekly soup kitchen for three or four decades, and started up that visitation project with shut-ins.

Was Betty still even going to that church, Connie wondered. She couldn't remember seeing her there in years. After Betty's husband died and she and her own husband divorced—several years after her children had gone and the last of the family pets had died—Connie only saw Betty when she was out at that bird feeder. Connie's attention was jolted back to the present by a pat on her hand.

"You were about to bid, Connie. You haven't gone to the birds too, have you—like Crazy Betty next door?" Connie turned to the woman sitting next to her, her best friend, Vicky, who drank coffee and gossiped with her for hours on end every weekday morning, and saw her for the first time in her life. She had been using "crazy" with Betty's name in her thoughts herself just now—but hearing it verbalized jolted and embarrassed her—and it made her feel little.

"Excuse me," Connie said, as she rose from her chair, pulled a coat off the hook near the kitchen door, and went out into her snow-dusted back yard. The old gate between the yards wouldn't budge, so Connie pushed herself between two boxwood bushes, sending clouds of snowflakes back into the air, and propelled herself into Betty Stapleton's yard.

It now was obvious why the cardinals were putting up such a fuss. Betty Stapleton was lying there, in just a thin house dress, at the base of the staked birdfeeder and on top of scattered birdseed. Connie went down on her knees, expecting the worst, but she could see that Betty was still breathing and nothing appeared to be broken. "Betty. Mrs. Stapleton, can you hear me?"

Betty murmured something indistinguishable, and her eyes fluttered. The cardinals were no longer swarming but had all lighted on branches, watching the scene with great interest.

"Here, you'll catch your death of cold. We must get inside and into something warm, and I'll call for some help."

Connie looked toward Betty's house. The kitchen door was ajar. Betty seemed to have become a bit more aware of her surroundings, so Connie helped her up and into the house, which was cold as ice. It was surprising how quickly a house could lose its heat when a door was left open in cold weather.

"Where's your thermostat, Betty?" Connie asked, as she helped the older woman into the living room. The house was a mess inside. Connie couldn't see any Christmas tree, and she suddenly reflected, with self-reproach, on how she had demanded that they add a third tree at her house this year, all loaded with expensive ornaments. "Here, let's wrap you in this afghan. I said, where can I turn up the heat?"

"It's broke," Betty mumbled, as she whispered her thanks to Connie for the afghan.

"Broken?" Connie asked. "Your heater's broken? When did that happen?"

"Oh, let's see. Two, three, uh—"

"Two or three days ago?" Connie asked in consternation.

"Oh, I'm trying to remember. I think it was back right after I finished helping Mr. Lyman with his broken leg."

"Mr. Lyman's broken leg? Why that was almost four years ago. You've been without heat for—?" Connie was flabbergasted, but then she formed an even worse thought. "Mrs. Stapleton, when was the last time you ate?"

"I, uh, well, I don't rightly know, Connie."

No wonder she had fainted out there in the yard. How long had Betty been living in these conditions, Connie wondered. And just next door all of this time.

It was then that Connie caught sight of the pictures on the mantle. There was one of children, but Betty hadn't had any children. When Connie looked closer, she saw that the photograph was of her own children—and of her own beloved, but long-gone cocker spaniel, Ginger. There her daughter and son were, happily

77

helping a much younger Betty fill that same bird feeder in the Stapleton's back yard, with Ginger in half leap beside Betty. It must have been taken by Mr. Stapleton, and from the looks of the children, it must have been taken while Connie and her husband were on that month-long Caribbean cruise and left the kids and pets with the Stapletons.

Tears came to Connie's eyes, as she turned and gently moved her neighbor toward the door. "We can't get you warm here, Betty. We'll go over to my house and call for some help from there."

Betty was putting up a bit of a resistance. "But the birds. I can't just leave them. The cardinals are back. Did you see them, Connie? The cardinals are back. And thoughts of Christmas not even over yet. And they're just the start; the cardinals are always the first to return. They need feeding. They need me."

"Yes, I saw them, Betty," Connie answered in choked-off words. "If I hadn't seen them, if they hadn't shown their concern for you, I wouldn't have known you were out there in the snow. Don't worry. I'll feed the birds while you're being checked over. And . . . and I'll be here when you get back, and we can feed them together then. In fact, it's gotten quite lonely over in my big house with the children gone now, and I've been wondering if you might like to move in with us for a while—you'd be only one yard away from your bird feeders then; we can see them from our breakfast room."

"And Betty," Connie said, urging her neighbor to focus on her face. "Thank you for the belated Christmas present?"

"Christmas present?" Betty asked, bewildered.

"Yes, thank you for restoring the sense of true community for me."

# Fading Star

"You didn't, Janice. Tell me you didn't."

"Yes I did, Sally. And so what? I don't see the problem choosing between a day with Dave and the kids at his mother's and a day at the spa."

"But . . . Thanksgiving?" Sally's breathy voice sputtered down the phone lines.

"All the better. The spa was nearly deserted. I didn't have to wait at any of the stations."

"Cool."

"Mom, Mom. Stevie's going to be late. He needs a ride." Janice's daughter flounced into the kitchen and grabbed up an apple for a bowl on the counter.

"Shut it, Carla. Can't you see Mommy's on the phone? The football field's only a mile and a half away. Steve can walk. It's good exercise for football."

Janice brushed her daughter away and, smoothening down the back of her terrycloth robe, plopped down in a kitchen chair and lit up a Virginia Slims.

"I'll tell ya, Sally. Life is just a pile of—"

"Mommy, Mommy. I thought the tree would be out and set up for decorating tonight. But it's not—" Carla was back at her mother's elbow.

Janice turned on Carla angrily. "I can't do everything all the time. Can't you see I'm on talking with Mrs. Jameson? You know what I've said about breaking into my conversations. Get those dishes from last night washed and get upstairs and do your homework."

Janice turned her back on her daughter, who moved, dejected, to the sink as Janice settled back on her haunches and took a big puff on her cigarette.

"You there, Jan?" Sally was about to hang up, assuming the connection had been broken.

"Yeah, I'm here, Sal. Just the chains rattling at me. The ball should show up at any minute," Janice answered. She dragged a full ashtray across the table, pushing aside bowls and milk glasses from breakfast.

"You were about to tell me—"

"Yeah, it's the doctor," Janice interjected. "You know I went in because of that lump I thought I found last week. Well . . . Gawd almighty, Carla, do you have to rattle those pans around like that? I can't hear myself think, let alone hear Mrs. Jameson. For Chris' sake leave them and go do your homework. You can do those with the dinner dishes. And you'd best be back down in a half hour to get dinner started."

Carla put the pans down as quietly as she could and turned to leave. A plaintive wail floated in from the direction of the family room.

"And take the baby upstairs with you. I'm sure she needs changed."

Carla lowered her head and changed direction. "Don't cry, Bethie. Carla's coming."

Alone again, Janice heaved a heavy "put upon" sigh, took a drag from her Virginia Slims, blew a stream of smoke out of the corner of her mouth, stubbed the cigarette out, and put the phone receiver back to her ear.

"Gawd, I think I'm going to explode, Sal. Not a moment of rest."

"Tell me about it," Sally responded, "My Dennis is a real demanding sonofabitch. But the doctor . . . you were saying about the doctor."

"Yes, I got this strange call. The receptionist sounded like a robot. She told me the doctor needed to talk to me about my tests . . . that I needed to come in."

"Oh, Janice, of course you need to—When do you need to—?"

"Tomorrow. I go back in tomorrow. I'm sure it's the insurance papers. You know how they were about that last time. If Dave's company only was . . . Oh, speaking of the ball, I hear mine driving into the garage. Gotta go."

When Dave entered the kitchen, Janice was standing at the sink, running water into a pan.

"Hi, Hon," Dave called out as he entered from the garage. He'd started with a big grin on his face, but that turned into a reserved, tentative smile as soon as he saw Janice. They'd been here before. "Aw, Hon. You're still in your bathrobe. It's nearly five, and—"

He knew he'd said the wrong thing as soon as the words were out of his mouth, but there was no way to stuff them back in.

"Chris' Almighty, Dave, of course I'm still in my bathrobe. Doing what I have to do around here, when would I have time to—? Oh, screw it." She brutally twisted the tap shut and turned and marched out of the room and upstairs. Dave heard the faraway sound of the bedroom door slamming.

Hours later, after Dave picked up Steve at football practice and returned in time to help Carla finish preparing dinner, to which Janice didn't make an appearance—after he had put Beth to bed while Carla and Steve cleaned up the kitchen—after Carla and Steve had finished their homework and hit the sack—and after Dave had rummaged, as quietly as he could, around in the attic for the Christmas tree, strings of lights, and decorations and somehow managed to assemble the tree in the living room, he mounted the stairs and pushed open the door to the master bedroom, the first time it had opened since Janice retreated up the stairs.

He found Janice sitting at a window—where he often found her at this time of night. She was dragging on a Virginia Slims, sipping Scotch from a juice glass, and staring up at the sky.

"What do you see, Janice?" Dave asked in his best attempt at a soothing, nonthreatening tone.

"Nothing," she answered in a manner that had Dave backing off. But she didn't see "nothing." She was watching her star, her special star. The star she had located in the firmament the night her mother had died, when Janice was just twelve. The star she watched for every chance she could since that night. Janice's dad had called it a Christmas star when Janice had shown it to him, a star that was most prominent during the early winter. It hadn't seemed too important to him. In fact, after Janice's mother died, her father just seemed to withdraw into himself—until he too seemed to fade away. However the star, this Christmas star that was more prominent in this season than any other, gave her some sort of grounding. Her own star. It twinkled brightly tonight, giving her strength. She'd been dismissive about the call from the doctor's office when she'd talked with Sally earlier. But she'd brought it up because she was going to ask Sally to go there with her. To give her strength. But the children, and Dave coming home early. Well, that ruined everything. But her star was still there, twinkling brightly. At least Janice had that.

"I know you're tired, hon," Dave said. "Maybe you should go to bed. I'll shower and be there in a minute. I can give you a backrub, and then, maybe—"

"Sure, right," Janice said dully. But she didn't move from where she was, or take her eye off her star, until Dave had gone into the bathroom and she heard the water running in the shower.

When Dave came out of the bathroom, the room was dark. He climbed into bed, finding that Janice was already there, turned away from him. He stretched out along her body, his thighs touching the back of hers, but his torso pulled away from hers, giving him room to get his strong hands in position to rub her shoulders and then move farther down her back and lower, working hard to interest and arouse her.

But Janice was already asleep. Or at least her eyes were shut tight, and she was completely nonresponsive. Dave eventually gave up, sighed, and turned over—his buttocks against hers—still trying to maintain a connection with this woman he loved and who had mothered his children. No response, however, and he sighed again as he drifted off into sleep. They had been here before, almost constantly in recent months.

\* \* \* \*

She'd been the last patient of the day. It was dark when she stumbled out to the parking lot, struggled with her car keys, and somehow got behind the wheel. Janice was trembling so hard she knew there was no way she was driving anywhere for some time.

For a long while she just sat there, staring up into the sky from the side window as twilight turned into night, the transition from murky day to darkest night coming quickly in early December. It was cold. They had predicted snow, but the sky was still clear.

Janice watched the stars begin to come out. She hungrily watched for her star, her very own star. When she saw it, it seemed to be dimmer tonight than last night. Somehow it didn't surprise her the star was dimmer. But she had hoped. . . . She wearily let her head fall against the cold pane of glass. And she cried, all alone in the parking lot, taking more than an hour to pull herself together well enough to drive the car and to face her family, to think of something she could say, some way she could deport herself so that they wouldn't know there was anything wrong.

When Janice arrived at home, Steve and Carla were already in their rooms, finishing up on the homework and preparing to go to bed. The kitchen was spotless, everything washed and put away. Even her ashtray was empty and had been washed. Dave was in the nursery, rocking Beth to sleep. No explanations were necessary. No one looked at her. No one asked her anything.

Janice went directly to the bedroom, changed into her nightgown, and went to the window. It had clouded over and was snowing now. No stars could be seen at all. Not even Janice's own star. For some reason she couldn't specifically identify, her tears started to flow again. Janice gave up on her vigil and went to bed. She was asleep before Dave managed to get Beth to sleep and quietly enter the room.

* * * *

The doctor had said she would receive a letter. They would try surgery, and she'd receive a letter giving her a surgery date and telling her how to prepare for it. He probably had conveyed what he had to say as sensitively as anyone could want under the circumstances, but it had all sounded so clinical and abrupt—and final—to Janice. The doctor wasn't the one who was dying. He clucked and clucked and look so forlorn and talked in such hushed and soothing tones when he'd told her. But he was trained to do this—and then to go home to a roast beef dinner and a night on the town with his wife. This is what had happened to Janice's mother. At this very age. How did one fight those inevitabilities?

The letter arrived three days before Christmas. Thank God, Janice thought, that the postman arrived, for a change, well before the kids got home from school. She'd hidden it in the linen closet, behind the pool towels. No one would be fiddling with those for six months. She couldn't open it. Not now. If she didn't open it, nothing had changed yet. Nothing was happening. Or so she told herself.

She didn't know why, but she needed to open it at the window, at night, after her star had come out. She had to open the letter when she could see her star still twinkling in the sky. But it had been overcast and had snowed every day since she'd gone to the doctors—not enough to close the city down, but enough to cover the nonpaved surfaces—enough to bring out the Christmas spirit of all of those around her.

After hiding the letter, Janice went into the living room and opened a new bottle of Scotch and poured herself the first of three hefty shots. She sat down on the sofa next to the Christmas tree, pushing aside the lights and boxes of decorations that still hadn't been moved to the tree. Carla had continued to wheedle at her about when they would trim the tree, but Janice was having nothing of that. She'd spent most of the time in her room. She was no actress, and she wasn't ready to say anything at all to the family.

While skipping on her third Scotch, Janice had lost enough of her reason to make the phone call. Dennis Jameson had been propositioning her for months. She'd been flattered at his attentions, but he had nothing in sex appeal compared with Dave, and she hadn't had any interest in even Dave for months—so Dennis hadn't seemed to be a threat to any of her desires. Besides, he was her best friend's husband. That alone had been enough for her to hold his advances off. But that resolve was no match for her mood or for her third Scotch or for the weather conditions that had separated her from her star for several days now.

When she called Dennis, he jumped at the chance to meet her at Dunigan's—the sooner the better.

The fourth Scotch at Dunigan's, as she and Dennis sat in a booth in the shadows toward the back of the barroom, was enough for Janice to not even twitch when Dennis's hand went under the hem of her skirt and started moving up her thigh. She was so numb that this was giving her no sensation at all.

What was she doing here? Why had she thought that this was an answer to anything?

Dennis was nibbling on her ear and whispering what he planned to do to her—not with her, but to her—and giving her directions to the motel he'd already booked into when Janice came out of her fog enough to mutter that she had to visit the ladies room and stumbled out of the booth, realizing this wasn't what she wanted at all. And if Dave wasn't an answer she was looking for, why the hell had she ever thought that Dennis Jameson would be?

She took her purse and her heavy sweater with her, and she walked right past the door of the ladies room and out through Dunigan's kitchen and circled back around to her car in the parking lot.

When she arrived home, Steve and Carla were already in bed. All of the lights were out in the living room except for the twinkling multicolored lights on the decorated Christmas tree. Dave was in his Laz-Y-boy, Beth cuddled in his lap, a child's version of *The Night Before Christmas* open on the floor beside the chair. Both were asleep.

They'd trimmed the tree without her. They already were learning to manage without her. She was fading away. Would she even be missed? And, if not, whose fault was that? She walked past Dave and Beth, moving quietly so not to wake them, and went to a window. She gazed up into the sky, clear for the first time in days. She felt the panic rising inside her until she found it. Yes, her star was still there. But it was dimmer than ever before. Definitely dimmer, she was sure. Her star, her life. Dimming. Her family. What in the hell had she been doing with her life?

Janice moved into the kitchen and started a pot of coffee brewing. While she waited for that to be ready, she returned to the living room, and, as carefully as she could, lifted Beth out of Dave's arms and took her up to the nursery. Beth was only half awake as Janice changed her and put a nightgown on her, but the baby was awake enough to put her arms around Janice's neck and nuzzle her face into the hollow she found there. Janice began to cry, but she managed with only low choking sounds until she'd gotten the baby settled.

Back in the kitchen, Janice tossed off two cups of coffee in quick succession and rummaged around in her purse, pulled out her last packet of Virginia Slims, and tossed those too. She padded into the living room, found the bottle of Scotch she'd opened earlier in the day, returned to the kitchen, and poured what remained in the bottle down the drain in the sink. A third cup of coffee and then she went upstairs. She was drawn immediately to the window. Yes, the star was still there. Maybe not as dim as she had thought earlier. She showered and powdered and brushed her teeth and then pawed through her drawers until she found and put on that skimpy nightgown Dave had brought home on their tenth anniversary, his blush and secret smile so disarming that she'd promptly found a babysitter while Dave called for reservations at the Hilton.

\* \* \* \*

Christmas Eve was awash with carols on the record player, cookies in the oven, popcorn on the stove, easy laughter, and overflowing love in Janice and Dave's household. Janice had never seen her husband and children happier or in such a glowing mood. If this was to be their last Christmas together, Janice was determined that it would be a memorable one. And she felt so ashamed, so happy and blessed and ashamed, that each and every one of her family members warmed to her with complete affection and trust. Not one of them hinted at what she'd been toward all of them for months. She didn't need to wait for Christmas for her present. These were her presents: her husband and children.

This would have been such a comfort to her if it wasn't so bittersweet. They didn't know what she knew. They took this as a "could be/maybe" that could go on forever. She knew otherwise. She suddenly had the urge to open the letter. Not because she wanted the inevitable process to begin, but because she needed some time to adjust to it before she told any of them. There couldn't be much time now before they all had to face it. The doctor had been very insistent that even to hold off on what was eating at her for any time at all, they would have to operate quickly. So, she had to read the letter tonight. She'd say nothing tomorrow, on Christmas Day, but soon thereafter she'd have to have prepared herself to tell the family.

The evening was drawing to an inevitable conclusion. They'd already put Beth to bed—she and Dave together—and soon Steve and Carla would have to go upstairs too. On a whim . . . no, not just a whim, really—on a sudden impulse of what she had to do,

Janice rose from the sofa and, taking Carla by the hand, pulled her over to the window.

"Come, there's something I need to show you, Carla."

"What? Where, Mom?" Carla asked when they had reached the window.

"There, up there," Janice said. "I need to point a star out to you, and I need you to always know how to find it."

"Where? I don't see it, Mom? It's just dark out there."

And so it was. Some stars were dimly evident, but not Janice's star. She searched hard for it, and she was so intent that she was clutching at Carla.

"Ow, Mom, that hurts," Carla said. And when Janice loosened her hold. "Where? I want to see it but where is it?"

"It's not there, honey," Janice said, trying to keep the clutch at her throat from conveying her to voice. "It's not there tonight, Carla. I don't know why, but I can't see it either. Not tonight. Maybe we can find it tomorrow night."

Janice almost wasn't able to get the words out. She didn't want to leave her family as her mother had, with just that one connection with her daughter, the winter-season star. That special star. That star that Janice could not find in the sky tonight.

Later, much later, when Dave was abed, blissfully snoring, Janice quietly left the bed and went to the linen closet. She'd gotten a small flashlight from her nightstand but still had trouble finding the letter. She suffered a moment of panic when it wasn't where she thought she'd tucked it, a flash of concern that someone else had found it, or that it had somehow been thrown away, or that it had never existed at all. But then, there it was, shifted to behind the pile

90

of blankets. She took it out, slit its edge slowly with her fingernail, and took it back into the bedroom, over to the window.

She extracted the letter from the envelope and began to read it. After she'd finished, she looked up into the sky, through the window, once more searching for her comforting star.

\* \* \* \*

"I'd sue them," Sally was screaming down the phone line. "I'd sue the pants off the bastards. To do that to you."

"I thought about it," Janice said. "But I don't think so."

It was night again and Janice was standing at the window beside the Christmas tree, now almost buried in Christmas wrappings. Dave and the kids were out in the kitchen making popcorn balls, something the family hadn't done for several years. Something Steve suddenly asked if they could do and Janice assented to if they could find the fixings. Obviously they had found what was necessary, because they were forming the balls and complaining good-naturedly at how hot the syrup was. Even Beth was so taken up in the activity that she didn't complain that she had been trapped in her high chair with only a candy cane sugar cookie for comfort.

"But why not? They didn't call you back, they just put it in a letter." Sally was saying, her voice still full of indignation. "They put you through all that worry and just sent a letter to tell you your X-rays had been mixed up with someone else's—that you didn't have any sign of cancer at all. I'd take them for all they've got."

Janice laughed. "I don't want what they've got, Sally. I want what I have. What I've always had and perhaps didn't appreciate nearly enough. I don't want to sue them. This mistake was probably the best Christmas gift I've ever received. Now, sorry, I wanted you

91

to know, but I've got a family having fun in the kitchen and I can't stand them having fun without me. Not tonight. Not ever again."

Janice clicked off the phone. But she didn't move to the kitchen immediately. She looked up into the sky through the window. And she saw it. Her star. Burning as brightly as ever. How had she ever imagined that it had faded away?

"Carla," she called out. "Wash your hands and come here for a minute. I want to show you something."

# Win, Win

I pursed my lips as I stood outside Corey's bedroom door and listened to his evening prayers.

" . . . and Shady our cat, and . . . and . . . make me win when we play the Tigers tomorrow afternoon. That'd be a great Christmas present."

I thought I'd drummed into Corey better than that that praying to win games was neither a good use of God or a sign of good sportsmanship. I was wavering there, wondering if I should go in right now to talk to him and reveal that I had been eavesdropping or try to bring the subject up the next day, when I tuned into what he then prayed for.

". . . . and make Tom win too, please. He's not as good at baseball as I am, and so he needs to win real bad."

All right, then, I thought, as I pulled away from the door. He had moved on to more selfless requests. But Corey's belated prayer for Tom was pretty impossible to satisfy, even for God. Tom was on the Tigers' baseball team. It was getting close to the end of the season and Corey's team was a contender for the championship. They certainly wouldn't take a tie with a basement-level team like the

Tigers as any sort of win—and there was no other way both of these friends could come out winners. I'd been dreading this all season, my son and my son's best friend meeting as opponents on the ball field.

Still, it was heartening to know that Corey was still concerned for the unfortunate Tom. The two had been the unlikeliest of best friends, coming, as they did from two entirely different worlds, and Corey being blest in academic and sports talent in almost diametrical opposition to all of Tom's unsuccessful strivings. But their friendship had survived, and even had flourished, through their kindergarten and elementary school years.

The afternoon of the baseball game proved quite surprising and not a little frustrating for Tom's team, as the Tigers—despite all the help that Tom's erstwhile fumbling at bat and in the outfield was giving Corey's team—were holding their own in the score. It was the bottom of the ninth, with the Tigers at bat and only one run down. For the first time that afternoon, though, Corey's team was pretty confident, because they had two outs and the ideal batter stood between the end of the game and the Tigers' best two sluggers. That batter, of course, was Tom, who hadn't connected with a ball, on either offense or defense, all afternoon.

If the Tigers had a clever coach, of course, this would have been the time to bring in a pinch hitter—that would have been the sensitive thing to do for all—but if their coach had been at all clever, they probably wouldn't have been in the league cellar to begin with. He left a trembling Tom standing, wobbling knees, at home plate, the weight of the game on his shoulders.

Watching from his third base position, Corey's eyes filled with tears from concern for his friend, and he stumbled out another prayer—a prayer that the Tigers' coach would take Tom off the batter's mound before he was totally humiliated. But nothing of the sort happened.

As always, Tom closed his eyes tight and swung widely at the first pitch. This is what Tom always did—he closed his eyes and fanned at all of the pitches. But this time something unusual happened. His bat connected with the ball—not solidly and not with any force on the ball, so that it slowly hopped, skipped, and jumped between first and second bases rather than soared for the fences. And it came up dead about halfway out toward right field.

Normally the ball would have been fielded easily, but everyone on the field, including Tom, was so surprised that he'd actually hit the ball at all, that everyone stopped dead in shock, including Tom. Tom was still standing at the plate, his eyes tightly shut, waiting for the call of strike, when he heard a familiar voice yell out over the crowd from the direction of third base.

"Run, Tom, run for first base. You hit the ball."

Tom ran down the baseline for dear life, arriving safe on first just before Corey's team mates had recovered their composure and the ball and had gotten it to the base.

The next batter up, the Tigers' pride and joy at the plate, did what no one had ever seen done before. He pounded the ball out straight to center field. But it didn't go over the fence for a clean home run; it hit a rock out in center field, bounced high, and went over the fence. The outfielders on Corey's team ran for the fence and, in a Keystone Cops panic, ate precious time in boosting one of their players over the fence to retrieve the ball.

With his team mates yelling at him across the field, Tom headed around the bases, with the slugger hot on his tail. Tom had pulled up lame in his unfamiliar dash for first base, though, and it was an increasingly painful ordeal to hobble around the infield bases. His movement became slower and slower, his hobble more pronounced, the pressing slugger more and more angry and vocally threatening, as Tom approached third base.

I saw Corey looking out to the field beyond the fence, where his team mate was having trouble locating the ball in the thick underbrush, and I could see the struggle going on within my boy from the changing expressions on his face. He was in position to catch the ball if it could reach him in time and tag Tom or the slugger out so that his team could either win or tie the game. But I could see how conflicted he was—just how much he wanted his best friend, Tom, to get to home, if only this one time in his Little League career.

Tom stumbled past him at third, and the slugger pulled up there, waiting for Tom to get out in front of him. But Tom collapsed to the ground, exhausted and his right leg now useless, fifteen feet beyond third. He struggled on, though, half crawling half pulling his body along with his elbows, determined to do all he could to make home.

I saw Corey's head swiveling back and forth, following the progress of the hunt for the ball out beyond center field and monitoring Tom's progress in the stretch of dirt between third and home.

And then I could see that Corey made a decision. My heart swelled and there was a roar of approval—even from the parents of

Corey's team mates around me, I was thrilled to note—as I saw him dash out from third, lift up Tom in his arms, and drag him home.

They never did find the ball out there in the brush beyond the center field fence, and I'm probably the only one who knows why—who knows that it was something that had to be for both Corey and Tom to be winners that day.

# Timing Out

"Guess what, Mom? We went all the way to Baghdad. Straight to Baghdad. Racing in our Humvees. No Problem. Whooie. Me and my buds are having the time of our lives. Ain't that great, Mom?"

"Yes, Craig, that's great. Does that mean you're coming right home?" Laura tried her best not to let her voice show the depth of her concern or her mixed feelings about this whole military deal.

"You shoulda seen 'em wavin', Mom. They all came out on the street to welcome us. We're freeing them, Mom. It'll all be over in no time. You shoulda seen them waving."

"That's wonderful, son. Ummm, do you think you'll be getting home by August? Lonny at the garage will have to get out for the harvest, and Mr. Dickerson was saying . . ."

"Gee, I don't know, Mom. There's word a few units will have to stay on for a while. We might—"

"You know what I can't quite understand. You're in the National Guard—what's the National Guard doin' so far from the nation? That's what I wanna know." Laura nearly burst out in tears. She'd coached herself to not go off like this. Certainly not at Craig for the few moments she'd get to talk with him from so far away. She knew her time with him on the phone was precious.

She took a drag on her cigarette to calm herself and then recoiled from that and tossed the cigarette in the sink. She'd been told to get rid of that crutch, as if that mattered any more. And she'd done all right—until Craig got sent off and that fighting had started.

"It's just that Mr. Dickerson can't hold your job forever, Craig. And you worked so hard to get it. It's just such bad timing. I—"

"Sorry, I gotta go, Mom. Guys are standing in line, and we have a time limit. You should get on the Internet, Mom. That's how the soldiers out here are keeping connected with their families. See Jim. He can get you fixed up."

"Sure, son. I'll see Jim—"

"Gotta go, Mom. Give my love to Charlene, will ya? Haven't gotten an e-mail from her yet."

"Sure, but hold on. There's something I need to tell you—"

"Gotta ring off, Mom. All the best. It's really great what we're doin' out here, Mom. Bye now."

Laura lowered the receiver with a trembling hand, turned to the sink, fished out the still-smoldering cigarette, and took another deep, evil drag.

"Bye, son. I needed to tell you about the cancer they found, though." This was spoken aloud and full of biting bitterness to the silent, dreary kitchen in the old log cabin up the dirt road in a rural valley of North Dakota. Tired lace curtains, split linoleum on the floor, and traces of sunlight on the warped cabinets shining through the chinks in the plaster between the logs. Still, somehow, she felt better, strangely comforted, for having said it out loud, for having named it—if only to herself for now.

* * * *

"He what?"

"I'm sorry, Craig. Mr. Dickerson had to let your job go to a new mechanic he brought in from over in Minot. He said he tried to hold it for you as long as he could, but he ran out of time; he's got a business to try to keep open. Life goes on here, you know; it doesn't hold still here for Iraq."

Silence.

"Do you think you'll be home for Christmas, Craig? This is really taking too—"

"Don't know, Mom. I doubt it. It's stringing out a little longer than they figured. There's a little resistance. But we're going to win. We're going to do this thing."

A short pause, with Laura turning away from the receiver so Craig couldn't hear her heavy sigh. And her hacking cough.

Then Craig again. "Mom, I'm wondering if Charlene's having trouble with her computer. My e-mails don't seem to be going through. And have you talked to Jim about getting you set up? I sure do miss you, Mom."

Laura couldn't breathe. She had to sit down. They told her there'd be moments like this in this stage. But she didn't think this was the sickness. At least not the physical sickness. She needed to see her boy, to hold him in her arms—the visceral need of connection. He couldn't know what "missing" really was—not like she knew; not like this monster that had a grip on her was forcing her to understand.

100

"No, I haven't talked to Jim yet. A computer's a little out of my budget at the—"

"Haven't you gotten the checks they were supposed to be sending you, Mom?"

"Yes, yes, of course." How to tell him where the money from the checks was going. She'd tried to tell him the last time, but this just wasn't the way—or the right time. Not across the miles like this. And not now. She'd been watching the news. He couldn't be having that on his mind just now. Maybe later, when everything over there was settling down. As surely it would. Sometime soon. Surely.

"Mom? Mom? You sound kinda hoarse. You got a cold or something? You keep the heat going in that old shed now, Mom. Cold weather's setting in and . . . well, I don't know how you can take the winters there anyway."

"Don't you worry about me, Craig. Just you stay safe and come home. If they have any Christmas leave on offer, grab it . . . for me . . . for my sake. OK? It's all I want for Christmas."

"Yeah, sure, Mom. That'd be great. Now, about Charlene—"

Laura held the phone to her ear for the longest time, willing it not to have gone dead. Desperate to hear his voice again, staying in connection, even if only over a phone line at great distance.

\* \* \* \*

"She what?"

"Charlene got married a week ago Saturday. I'm sorry, son. I thought she would have told you. It was that new mechanic at Dickerson's garage. I spoke to her at the church for a minute afterward. She said time was flyin', and she couldn't just put her life on hold forever."

Silence.

"I'm real sorry. I know you shouldn't be hearing anything that will get you down right now. I read the papers. I know you're having it rough there. Believe me, I'd do all I could not to be conveying bad news from home."

If only he knew how far she'd gone with that, she thought, wrapping her coat tight around her chest. She'd used the last of the wood two days ago and it was fixing to snow tomorrow. It was the middle of the night now and there was a ring around the moon. That always meant there'd be a storm. But it had come down to a choice between treatments, food, or heat. She'd managed two of them, at least. Oh, God, why couldn't her son be coming home? What in the hell were they doing over there anyway?

"Well. . . . I guess you're not going to get that computer and learn how to connect to e-mails, are you?" It was almost an accusation, his disappointment knifing down the phone lines and slicing into her heart. A flash of anger and hurt shot through her too. She hadn't had electricity for a month, so e-mails were sort of a bad joke just now. She'd laugh if she weren't trying so hard to stifle a sob. Instead, she jagged into a coughing fit. It wasn't his fault; he just wanted to have whatever connection they were to be allowed. It just wasn't the connection she needed herself.

"Mom? Mom? Did you get that cold I told you not to get?"

"Yes, I guess I did. I guess I just can't do anything right when you're not here. Can't you come—?"

"Ah, shit, Mom. They're motioning me to give up the phone. Time's up, Mom. Merry Christmas, ya hear? Time's up. Love ya. Bye."

Click.

Time's up. Time's up. Yes, just about right, Laura thought bitterly. And then she did break down . . . into open-mouthed, hunched-against-the-counter, see-your-frozen-breath icy sobs, huddled there, wrapped in her winter coat in the "warmest" room in her cabin, soon overtaken by wracking coughs.

\* \* \* \*

Moving up the road into the valley from the bus stop as fast as he could in eight inches of crunchy snow. His ragged breath steaming, thinking wild thoughts, searching for the chimney of the cabin. Craig was cold, nearly frozen stiff. He'd thought it was cold in Baghdad that January. But Baghdad wasn't anything like North Dakota in the winter. He'd been gone too long. His body had forgotten how to adjust to the cold of a North Dakota winter— assuming anyone ever could.

He had to see the chimney, to see the curling smoke of home, to know it wasn't as bad as he feared. Phil from down at the store had called him and told him it was bad with his mother, and he'd gone to his sergeant, and they'd furloughed him home. They'd said they could give him a little time; all he needed to do was ask. Time. A little time.

There, wasn't that the house? But, no, it couldn't be. That one looked abandoned. But, yes, yes, that was the house. How could he have forgotten so quickly? Home.

But, there wasn't any smoke coming out of the chimney.

Craig tried moving faster in the snow drifts and only managed to fall down and get snow inside his boots.

Hurry, hurry, hurry. And then just sit and ponder and wonder and succumb to the reproofs. The house was empty, deserted, and cold as an ice floe and had obviously been that way for some time—a solitary Arctic ice floe. Craig sat there in the kitchen, huddled in his coat, feeling the snow melting, ice cold, through his socks. Looking at the tired lace curtains and the split linoleum and the warped cabinets, but not really seeing them. Time had run out. She wasn't here. Why hadn't she told him on the phone? His eyes focused on the telephone. But, of course, she'd tried to tell him. He knew that now, now that he concentrated for the first time on what she was saying—and what she hadn't been saying. She'd sat right here where he was sitting, talking to him on the phone, trying to tell him how fleeting time was. She had been reaching out, wanting to touch him, and all he'd been able to think of was playing savior soldier half a world away and wondering why she couldn't be bothered to get on the Internet and connect with him. Connections could time out just like that while you're off crunching up time to little or no effect.

Craig snapped alert to the ringing of the telephone.

"Craig, that you? Phil from down at the store. Hoped you'd be there. Your mom's up here at the house. We came down there and brought her up last night. She hadn't told anyone just how bad it was over there. Get yourself on over here, boy. You ask me, it's time you guys stopped spinning your wheels over there and were brought on home for good. There's enough needs doin' and savin' and savoring right here."

Craig let out a sob and lurched for the door. Time. Just a little more time, probably. But every minute precious and fleeting now.

# Moment of the Deer

"You know, the chocolate disks covered with gold foil."

"We don't have those."

"You know, the ones made up like gold coins; they have them every Christmas."

"It's Christmas Eve. We sold out on those more than a week ago."

"I mean my son decided the family could come tomorrow after all at the last minute, and we have those for the grandchildren every year they visit. Well, might you know where I could—?"

"No, I don't," Nancy cut in, anxious to move the line along. "We sold out of those last week." She had, in fact, seen those a day or two before over at CVS, but there was no reason why she should be sending business over there. There was no reason why she should have to work on Christmas Eve at all. People could jolly well think ahead on their needs.

The man just sort of zoned out of her attention. Her gaze had been arrested by an elderly women with scraggly gray hair and in what looked like an overcoat over a nightgown and scruffy slippers wandering around in aisle two. When Nancy looked back across the cash register, the man looking for the chocolate coins was gone, to be replaced by a weary-looking young woman with a baby in her arms and a fat toddler pulling at her leg. The woman had put a can of infant formula on the conveyer belt and was rummaging around in her purse, saying she thought she had a store coupon for that. Her toddler had his chubby hand in a can of candy canes on the counter and had pulled one out.

"Should he be doing that?" Nancy asked sharply, an edge to her voice. The nerve of some people loading their fat kids up on candy, she thought. She really didn't approve of the store putting out things out there to tempt the brats anyway.

"Oh, sorry," the woman said. "Well, all right, Mikey," she went on to say to the toddler. "But just because it's Christmas."

"Excuse me," a rather dreamy, confused voice drifted into Nancy's hearing as she was finishing ringing the young woman up. "Can you tell me where the Tums are? I can't seem to find them, and my Ralph is—"

"Right over there on aisle three," Nancy said with a bit of exasperation in her voice to the old woman in the overcoat. "Right where they've always been," she muttered sotto voce as the elderly woman drifted away.

The shift from hell, Nancy thought. She was glad when this one would be over. She hadn't really had any plans for Christmas Eve, but no one should have to work an evening shift on this day.

At last the shift was over, but Nancy's irritation increased as she was driving home and found she had to detour around the main street between her work and her apartment because they had a drive-by Christmas lights display along that stretch of the road. She hadn't

107

thought about that being there and had reached a point where she'd have to take a winding, rural road around the town or backtrack to get to the highway going through on the other side of the town.

She turned onto the rural road and sped up a little faster than she should to make up for the lost time the detour would cause.

She rounded a curve and went into shock as the headlights picked up a large deer standing still in the middle of the road. Deer and woman froze, panicked eyes latched onto panicked eyes. And, as the deer leaped in one direction, Nancy's car lurched in the other direction, and she went down into a ditch and up into a tree, the tail of car still on the apron of the road.

She sat there, dazed from having her head bounce off the side window. The hit wasn't hard enough to set off her airbag, but she saw stars and felt the ooze of blood at her temple.

She was bathed in the headlights of another car, and a man and woman, dressed in evening apparel, appeared at the side of the car, almost instantly, giving her very concerned looks as she rolled the window down.

"Are you all right?" the man asked?

"Are you hurt?" the woman chimed in.

"A deer. It was a deer," Nancy said, rather dumbly.

But right at that moment the beam from a strong flashlight appeared at the corner of the passenger side of Nancy's car, revealing that she'd gone off the edge of the road right next to a driveway.

"I heard the crash," a man was calling out. "Anyone hurt? Oh, that doesn't look too good. Here, let me help you up to the house and we'll see about that gash . . . and about your car. It'll have to be moved or there'll be another crash here."

"I'll stay with her car until a wrecker comes," the first man said.

"I'll go call the Mitchells on my cell phone and tell them we'll be late to the party," his wife called out as she started back to their car. "We'd better leave our headlights shining on her car until the wrecker gets here so anyone else coming around the curve can see it in time."

As the man whose driveway Nancy plowed across and who identified himself as Steve Brandon helped her up to his house, he was asking her if she was in pain anywhere else, but she said she didn't think so. "Still, we'd best call Doc Watson—they live a couple of driveways down—and ask him if he can come over and take a look at you. Do you have AAA?"

"Eh, no, no, I'm sorry, I don't," Nancy answered. She was still feeling a little woozy.

"Guess I'll call Joe Timberman then," Steve said. "He's got the Exxon station up on Maple. Maybe he can bring his truck over and take your car over there at least for tonight. When that's taken care of, I'll drive you home."

When they entered the house, Steve's wife was there, looking concerned and putting her arms around Nancy and helping her to a chair between the fireplace, where a fire was flickering, and a lighted Christmas tree. It was clear that Steve had been assembling toys for young children hopefully abed and at least pretending to be asleep in anticipation of Christmas morning.

"Oh, you can't drive me home. You're—" Nancy muttered.

"I was figuring I'd be up half the night getting this together anyway," Steve said with a laugh. "Another hour or two won't matter much."

"Here, dear," Steve's wife said as she returned from the kitchen. "Here is a mug of hot chocolate and a few Christmas cookies. I called Doc Watson. He was at his daughter's house, but he said he'd be over within a half hour. I'll go call Joe Timberman now."

"It looks worse than it is," Doc Watson said as he finished cleaning the gash on Nancy's temple. "A butterfly bandage should do for now. But maybe you should go into the hospital in the morning to get that checked out. I can meet you there and help you through the process, if you like."

Nancy was murmuring her thanks as she heard the sounds of activity out on the road. She stood and went to the window and saw that a wrecker had arrived and two men were hooking up the tail end of her car to a hoist. The couple in the evening apparel were still there, with the headlights of their car beamed on hers.

Movement caught Nancy's attention out of the corner of her eye, and she turned her gaze to where, bathed in moonlight and standing in a majestic stance in a clearing at the edge of the forest—and peering straight into her face—was a deer. Perhaps the same deer she'd already encountered.

They were both frozen there for a long moment, eyes latched onto eyes. Nancy's eyes teared up, though, in sudden recognition that something had touched her deeply inside on this Christmas Eve, and when she had cleared the haze of her vision, the deer had disappeared.

# Time for Grace

I'm not sure when it first hit me that she was no stranger to me, and it took several weeks longer to realize the entire disturbing truth.

But why am I awake and why did I wake to this thought? I don't think I was dreaming anything about this. Or was I? I do remember something like this in a dream, but was that just now or last week? Get a grip, girl. Either snap awake or drift back off into sleep. Angel has buried her furry little muff into my neck. She's tickling me with her whiskers, which is going to make it very hard for me to get back to sleep.

But it wasn't Angel who woke me up. I'm clear on that. It was the sound of a car sliding on the street outside. The snow must be accumulating on the street surfaces now. It's going to be a rough night—and even rougher commute for people tomorrow. I don't want to think about having to go out in that tomorrow morning.

I burrow down under the comforter, and Angel goes underneath as well and stretches along my legs and kneads the flesh of my thigh, demanding attention. I should be blissfully comfortable. But I'm not. It isn't just the cat or the car sliding on the street outside that has me awake. I'm wondering where Grace is and if she's found someplace to keep warm and dry. I can feel Angel's heart racing. Cats must be able to sense the change in the weather—and its effect on people. She must know that the temperature is dropping outside and snow is falling and that this somehow makes the night more dangerous. But maybe that's *my* heart that's racing. I turn to the other side and pull the covers up, but Angel moves with me and, crawling up my body, digs in under my chin.

I'm going to have to stop thinking about Grace if I'm going to get any sleep tonight. But why did hearing a car skid remind me of Grace? Ah, yes, it was seeing that car being towed in the lane beside me as I came home from shopping for Christmas presents this evening. It looked just like Grace's car. But I don't want to think about Grace. It's the Christmas season. I want to think about that— my favorite holiday season.

Let's see. What has to be done at the office first thing in the morning? The thought is interrupted by the sound of another car skidding, this time the sound ending in a metallic thud—but it just sounds like a hit on the curb at the curve up the street. The sound is echoed by a whimper from Angel. I sure hope that Grace has found shelter. I wonder if she will have gone far from where I left her off this afternoon—beside her car. It was unbelievable what she had crammed into that car. I don't see how anyone can actually live out of a small car like that.

Was the first time I realized it was her when I was strolling down Main Street on my way to having a coffee and reading the paper at the Paper Moon café? I turned the corner onto Main, and there she was, shuffling along behind a grocery cart filled with bits and pieces of this and that. It wasn't so much that she was dirty, but that she looked so like a rag muffin in those mismatched, out-of-season clothes and the straggly hair that hadn't seen a perm in I don't know how long. I wouldn't even have noticed her if she hadn't given me that shy, little smile. She was actually making eye contact. It wouldn't have happened at all if I'd had time to see her coming. I could have avoided it all, if I hadn't been surprised and made eye contact myself.

How do I feel about that? What if I hadn't ever made that eye contact the first time I'd seen her? As it was, my trip to the café was ruined. I'd had to duck into the needle shop after I'd made eye contact with Grace on the pretense that that was where I was headed in the first place. And then I couldn't very well have gone on to the open-air café; she might still have been shuffling around out on the street. I don't know if I'd slipped and given a look of horror when our eyes had locked—or if she'd seen me do it. But the embarrassment of being caught off guard like that . . . . It just made me *so* uncomfortable. We'd been talking about the homeless in Sunday School just the week before, and I'd been so self-assured about my attitudes about these people.

I close my eyes tight and try to clear my mind of all thoughts. This has just got to work.

I must have drifted off to sleep, because time seems to have passed before I am jolted awake. I have no idea what woke me this time. Angel is gone now. Who knows where she must have found more security. I must have failed her somehow as her refuge. Yeah, I'm good at that. Now, I wonder what made me think of that? I turn over again, and then I sit straight up in bed and fluff the pillows.

No, that wasn't the first time. The first time was a few days before at the grocery store. She was sitting on the bench near the front entrance with her shopping cart. That must have been where she got the shopping cart. I wonder whether people steal a lot of their carts and what the store does about that.

I flop back down on the bed in disgust and pull the covers over my head. Who the heck cares? Oh, why can't I get to sleep. There's *so* much I have to do tomorrow. And I'd promised to take Grace back to the free clinic for her results during my lunch—but only because I also was taking Mrs. Wilkins to check her blood again. I'm not sure how I managed to get myself roped into transporting Grace; working with Mrs. Wilkins should be enough. And there's so little time for this at Christmas.

Did I see any sort of shelter around where I left Grace off this afternoon? The snow is going to be drifting by tonight. The TV news tonight said a freeze had been declared until tomorrow morning, that the snow might turn to freezing rain. I wonder if Grace's car will be shelter enough for her. But then, if that car I saw being towed last evening was hers—

As if on cue, there's a strong gust of wind outside that sends the trees rustling, and the first drops that sound much heavier than just snow hit the window. They sound like they're big—and cold. I turn on the light on my nightstand to check the time, and just then the electricity chooses to go out. A great silence, except for the tinkling sound of ice crystals hitting the window. Oh, great, the alarm's going to be off. I reach over for the flashlight on my nightstand, and, of course, it falls into the narrow crevice between nightstand and wall. I fish it out, open the drawer, feel around for my travel alarm, and set it in the wavering light of the flashlight. I'll have to change the batteries in the flashlight in the morning. In fact, I wonder how fresh the batteries in the travel alarm are? I wonder where I've stashed fresh batteries. I wonder if Grace has a flashlight in that grocery cart of hers. O-h-h, I moan, and flop back onto the bed and pull the covers up. Shutting my eyes tight again and trying to purge my mind of all thoughts. It had worked before; it's going to have to work again.

Does Grace have anything warm enough and waterproof to wear tonight?

"Oh, it's no use," I yell to the empty apartment. "OK, just bring it on." With that permission, the thoughts of Grace flood into my mind. What was she wearing on her feet when I last saw her? Would I have become involved at all if I hadn't substituted for Brenda at the church soup kitchen Thanksgiving Day and Grace had actually spoken to me as I filled her plate, trying my best not to make eye contact, knowing then that I'd seen her before and unwillingly exchanged smiles? She talked to me; she talked directly to me. Would she have dared do that if I hadn't been surprised into making that first eye contact and being tricked into returning that first shy smile? What am I thinking? Why shouldn't she smile at me when we pass on the street and thank me when I've filled her dinner plate? What's wrong with me? We had been friends; why wouldn't she have the right to speak to me?

The wind comes up and the branches of the oak hit against the window next to my bed. I give up, flounce out of bed, wrap myself tightly in my warm, quilted robe, and pad down the hall to the kitchen for a cup of coffee. I turn on the light in the kitchen and nothing happens. Naturally; the electricity's off, dummy. That means no coffee, either. Not even any coffee, I whine in my mind. I'm beginning to really feel sorry for myself. Well, guess what, there's no hot coffee for Grace, either. So, just stop your selfish whimpering.

Yes, my friend. Well, more an acquaintance, really. But not just another stranger on the street. That was the real shock. And I'll bet Grace knew back there on Main Street when she smiled. She probably even knew it when she saw me avert my eyes and scoot by her at the grocery store. It didn't hit me until I saw her in the free clinic the other day when it was my turn to take old Mrs. Wilkins in for her blood test. She'd been there, sitting patiently in the waiting room. We exchanged looks a couple of times while Mrs. Wilkins was back getting her blood drawn, and finally Grace worked up the courage to voice a tentative, "Celeste? You *are* Celeste Murray, aren't you?" And then it all flooded back to me. Of course this woman was familiar; we'd worked in the same office for nearly four months. We'd gone to lunch together on more than one occasion. This was Grace what's her name, Grace Jordon.

I must have been in shock, because I didn't respond immediately, upon which Grace seemed to shrink back into her chair. She probably didn't know why she had taken that last swing at the social barrier that had been carefully built between us. I certainly didn't know; at that moment, it was a revelation that I'd ever had contact with anyone on the other side of the bar, let alone a past friendship, even if only a short office acquaintanceship. In that brief, awkward moment, it had all flooded back to me. We'd thought of Grace as the bad news girl. Everything seemed to go wrong around her in the office, and she seemed to be in a daze much of the time.

116

Sometimes she reacted in strange ways, and sometimes she didn't respond at all. I know some of the rest of us thought she was a drinker. And there was a rumor that she was living out of her car. She certainly dressed and smelt like she did. And then one day she just didn't show up at all. When I finally got up the courage to ask, I was told simply that they'd had to let her go. They didn't give a reason, and I didn't ask for a reason. I hadn't even cared enough to ask for a reason. And now, there she was, in the waiting room of the free clinic. And I was here too, trapped until Mrs. Wilkins came back from her blood test.

All of this must have flashed through my mind in less than a second—and I must have said something back to Grace, because the receptionist was coming over.

"Oh, do you know Grace?"

"Umm, yes," I responded quietly through a weak smile. "Yes, yes, we've met."

"Well, do you think you could take her back to Grant Avenue, just down from the library, when you leave then? She's been sitting here for some time and says she doesn't think she can get over there without a ride. We did do some tests, and she probably is still a little weak from that."

What could I say? "Yes, certainly, I could do that. Mrs. Wilkins lives over in that area too." And that had led to further rides, both ways, the last two weeks, as they did test after test, trying to find out what problems Grace had that they actually could help solve. I felt trapped. I had so much to do to prepare for Christmas; I didn't have time for Grace and these trips to the doctor's. And as trip built on trip, I saw flashes of the old Grace I had once known, and I couldn't, for the life of me, think why I had cared so little about why she was fired from our office and what had happened to her afterward.

The snow isn't letting up a bit; if anything it has become thicker and is building. Normally this is perfect sleeping weather, and just now, just as I am about to return to bed, the lights come back on. I'd forgotten to turn the Christmas tree light off, and there it is, framed in the doorway to the living room, Twinkling its multicolored lights at me.

My mind isn't really on the tree, though. All that I can think of is that cup of coffee; I need that cup of coffee. No, that's not the only thing I am thinking of. I'm thinking that I'm going to be having a nice, hot cup of coffee and Grace isn't. Where's Grace? It that park where I left her on Grant this afternoon have anything in the way of a shelter? I can't remember. And was that her car I'd seen being towed this evening? If so, she likely didn't have any shelter at all. I kept telling myself that this was her choice—a choice she had made and had every right to make. But I was just kidding myself. I hadn't ever asked her that question—whether she lived that way by choice or by chance. I'd spent no real time on Grace at all, despite those trips back and forth to the doctor's office. I didn't even know what her malady was and whether she was getting better. She certainly had a hacking cough earlier today.

I fill the basket of the two-cup coffeemaker with grounds, and then I hear the meow. I turn around, and there's Angel. I call her to me, and she just gives me a disgusted look and strolls back down the hall to who knows where. I don't know why, but that just makes all of the strength go out of my arm and I drop the coffeemaker basket on the kitchen counter and sink down on a kitchen stool. I'm close to tears. But then Angel returns to the kitchen, walks over and weaves through my legs, and then plops down on her cushion in the corner of the room.

I look up and there are those twinkling lights of the Christmas tree. I am mesmerized by the lights. I pull myself out of my stupor and shove the small coffeemaker to the back of the counter, open the cabinet below, and drag out the twelve-cup coffeemaker and a thermos jug.

A half hour later, I'm pulling up to the curb at Grant Avenue. There she is, over by that big tree, huddled behind a dripping grocery cart, burrowed into the snow, covered by a tarp slick from the freezing rain and with a film of white snow rising half way up its surface from the ground.

"Grace? Grace, I brought you some coffee."

"What? Who? Celeste, is that you?" She emerges from her improvised cocoon and sits there, looking dumbly at my thermos of coffee. I look at the thermos as well. What a dumb idea. She's sitting there, soaked by freezing rain, and all I've brought is coffee.

"Yes, it's me. Come on get up. We're going home. The shopping cart should fit in the back of van."

"What? I don't understand. Home?"

"I don't understand either, Grace, but we'll work it out. We'll work something out. Come on, you're frozen nearly stiff. You'd said earlier today you wished you could see the Christmas tree I'd talked about putting up. Well, I want someone other than me and the cat to enjoy it too. Climb aboard."

# Olivia Stowe

Olivia Stowe is a published author under different names and in other dimensions of fiction and nonfiction and lives quietly in a university town with an indulgent spouse and two demanding Siamese cats.

www.cyberworldpublishing.com